RANGER BRAVERY

TEXAS RANGER HEROES

LYNN SHANNON

RANGER BRAVERY

God is within her, she will not fall;

Psalm 46:5

ONE

A scream rent the air.

Piper Jensen skidded to a stop on the running path cutting through the nature preserve. Thick tree branches overhead blocked out most of the lingering sunlight as day gave way to dusk. Long shadows lurked in the woods. The creek bubbled, tumbling over rocks as it rushed toward the lake, its banks full after the thunderstorms from the last few days. She sucked in a breath. The air was fragrant with pine and damp earth. She scanned the immediate area. Nothing.

Had she imagined the scream? Maybe it was the cry of a wild animal. This area of Texas had cougars.

Beside her, Moxie lifted his ears. The golden lab was a terrible guard dog but had excellent hearing. His nose twitched. Piper's hand drifted to the concealed weapon in her backpack. Overly cautious? Perhaps. If it was an animal, chances were it would stay far away from her.

But what if it was a person? Someone in trouble?

Goosebumps rose on Piper's skin. It'd been five months since she'd returned to Rock Fort. The small town tucked in the corner of the Texas Hill Country was known for its laid-back atmosphere, pioneer museum, gorgeous hiking trails, and stunning fields of spring bluebonnets. But she'd witnessed firsthand the darkness that lurked under the surface of that picture-perfect atmosphere. The summer before college, Piper had been assaulted and nearly killed while dropping off groceries to her mentally ill mother.

She was a strong woman, but the attack almost broke her. She'd scraped and clawed her way out of a dysfunctional childhood filled with instability and chaos. Against the odds, and despite the catty words of the town gossips, she graduated high school with top grades and was set to start college in the fall. Everything was finally going right. And then... it all came crashing down.

She could still remember the days after the attack. The quiet whispers behind her back, the stares when she walked through town. The PTSD. Piper jumped every time someone touched her. Her heart raced at every bump or loud noise. She couldn't sleep. Couldn't eat. Nothing made it better. Not even when her assailant was killed during a shootout with the police while resisting arrest.

Three weeks after being attacked, Piper blazed out of town in a rickety Ford, vowing never to return. The relief she felt seeing the town disappear in her rearview mirror was indescribable. For the first time, she could breathe.

Could be who she wanted to be. Unfortunately, her need to escape came at a cost.

Jackson Barker. Her first love.

They'd attended high school together, but it wasn't until the summer before college they fell in love. The romance between them was sweet and innocent and everything she'd dreamed of as a young girl hiding under the covers of her bed reading romance books while her mother screamed at the latest ingrate living in their home.

Breaking up with Jackson was one of the hardest things she'd ever done. Doing it in a note... well, it'd been cowardly. She hadn't had the emotional wherewithal to face him and end things in person. Nor did she trust Jackson wouldn't try to talk her out of it. He'd done everything possible to support and love her, especially after the attack, but Piper couldn't see a way to make their relationship work. Not with her past, her stack of problems.

Jackson had always been far too good for her.

Water in the creek rushed over rocks and tumbled down the pathway cut through the woods. Piper held her breath, her gaze scanning the tree line, searching for any sign of danger. What had she heard? A scream? Or was it all in her imagination?

Had her PTSD returned? A shudder rippled over her skin. She hadn't had an episode in years, but returning to Rock Fort had drudged up memories. Especially since it'd been an unexpected move. Her older sister, Ava, a single mother, had a car accident. She'd broken her pelvis and shattered her right knee. Piper had moved back home to help care for her niece and nephew while her sister recovered from her injuries.

Another scream ripped through the air. Closer this time. Unmistakably human.

Filled with terror.

Piper's pulse beat out a steady rhythm while on her run, but now it skyrocketed. She pulled her handgun free of her backpack. The cool metal was familiar. Seven years in the Bismarck Police Department had honed her skills as an investigator, expertise she now used on a daily basis as a detective for the Rock Fort Sheriff's Department. A breeze rustled the leaves and chilled the sweat gathered on her brow.

Moxie whimpered, his tail tucked between his legs. He glanced at Piper with concern.

She couldn't take him with her. There was no way to know what she was walking into, and the dog was a liability. Moxie would pull on his leash and take her down or he'd alert a potential attacker to their location. She needed focus and both hands free. Piper quickly secured his leash to a tree and patted his head. "I'll be right back, boy."

She slipped off the running trail into the woods. The screams had originated up ahead. At least one person— possibly more—crashed through the brush. The ruckus carried on the sweet spring air. She knew these woods. Had spent hours playing in them as a child. There was a field several yards away. It sounded like the individual was coming from that direction.

Piper pulled her cell phone from her pocket. No

signal. That wasn't unusual for this area of the nature park, but it was incredibly frustrating. She had no way to call for backup. Piper shot off a message to her supervisor, Sheriff Derek Martinez. Sometimes a text would go through even if a call didn't. It was a long shot though.

Fear clamped her stomach, but she ignored it. A childhood of trauma and a career in law enforcement had cemented her ability to separate her emotions from her actions. She pressed forward.

Piper's tennis shoes made no sound against the still-damp leaves. A mosquito buzzed her ear. The sweat coating the back of her exercise shirt grew cold as wind fluttered the strands of her honey-blond hair. Her heart thumped against her chest and she kept her gun at the ready. The sound of the brook faded as she maneuvered deeper into the woods. The crashing noise grew louder. Someone was definitely running through the woods.

There. A flash of yellow against the green and brown backdrop. Piper raised her gun. "Police! Freeze!"

The figure paid her no heed. It barreled toward Piper, bursting out of the brush like a horror movie.

A woman. Blonde hair, wide eyes.

Blood stained the front of her torn dress.

"Help..." she gasped. Stumbled toward Piper on bare feet.

Instinctively, Piper lowered her weapon and caught the woman one second before she tumbled to the ground. The woman sagged as if every ounce of energy had been drained from her body. Judging by the amount of blood coating her dress, it'd been adrenaline and sheer strength of will that'd gotten her this far.

Piper lowered her to the ground. Her hands became slick with blood.

Had the woman been shot? Stabbed? Something horrible had happened.

"Who did this to you?" Piper asked, her gaze shooting to the trees.

Nothing stirred.

"I... I..." The woman shook violently. She was losing blood too quickly.

Piper ripped off her exercise shirt and pressed it against the worst of the wounds. "It's going to be okay." The words were spoken calmly, although anxiety pulsed through her veins. Whoever this woman was, she was gravely injured. With no way to call for EMS, the chances of her surviving this attack were growing slimmer by the second. Still, it wasn't nothing. And Piper would do whatever she could to save the woman's life. "Who did this to you?"

The woman moved her mouth, but no sound came out. Tears leaked from her eyes. Clear blue eyes. The color of a Texas summer sky. Piper knew she'd see them again. In nightmares. Haunting her.

"Tell me your name."

Again, the woman's mouth moved. Her breath was faint. Piper leaned closer to hear.

"Elena."

"Hi, Elena." Piper smiled at her, although inside she

was crying. She pressed harder on the woman's wound. Blood seeped from the others. She mentally cursed herself for not carrying a first aid kit in her backpack. Rookie mistake. She was only going for a five-mile run. Her house was close. If she didn't return in the next twenty minutes, her sister and the kids would start looking for her.

Could Elena last twenty minutes? Piper didn't think so. *God, please guide my hands and my words.*

"Elena, I'm Piper." She removed one hand from Elena's stomach to open her backpack. She'd tucked a towel inside to wipe Moxie's paws before letting him back into her SUV after their run. Her fingers shoved aside her water bottle and dug for the bottom. "I'm going to get you out of here, okay?" Victoriously, she pulled the terry cloth from her bag and added it to the other wound. She took Elena's hand and used it to apply pressure. "Hold this here."

A twig snapped.

Piper's head shot up. Fresh adrenaline spiked through her veins. She grabbed her weapon and held it out in front of her. Leaves rustled. Her heart rate increased as she used both hands to steady her gun. Someone was in the woods.

Elena's attacker? Was he coming to finish the job?

He'd have to go through Piper first.

The hair on the back of her neck rose as she sensed a presence nearby. Her gaze scanned the forest, but the waning sunlight cast long shadows. He was there. She knew it but couldn't see him. A monster hiding in the dark.

And he was close.

TWO

Texas Ranger Jackson Barker ducked under the crime scene tape. Temperatures had dropped with the sun, leaving the night air crisp. Stars blotted the sky surrounding a full moon. Under normal circumstances, he'd admire the view. But not tonight. The fifty-mile drive to Rock Fort had been spent preparing himself for the task ahead. Viewing a crime scene was part of the job, but coming face-to-face with his very first sweetheart... well, that wasn't something a man did every day.

Jackson's gaze scanned the crowd of deputies, finally landing on the sheriff near the perimeter. His long strides ate up the distance. "Derek."

Sheriff Derek Martinez broke away from the deputy he was speaking to and intercepted Jackson. Forty, with dark hair graying at the temples, he'd started his career decades ago with the Rock Fort Sheriff's Department. His laidback nature made it easy to trust him, but underneath that good-old-boy nature was a sharp intellect.

Jackson had known him for decades, since he was a young boy. Derek had been a mentor in high school and had inspired Jackson's own career in law enforcement.

"Jackson." Derek greeted him with a warm smile. "Thanks for coming so quickly. I know you're working overtime since Cole is still on medical leave."

Cole Donnelly was another member of Company A. Normally Rock Fort was his jurisdiction, but he'd been shot in the shoulder several weeks ago while protecting his now-fiancée, Olivia. The criminals involved had been caught, and Olivia was safe, but it would take months for Cole to fully recover. Jackson was filling in for him.

"I'm happy to help snag a criminal off the streets." Jackson shook Derek's outstretched hand. "It's good to see you."

They hadn't seen each other or spoken in over a year. An oversight on Jackson's part. He was terrible at returning phone calls when knee deep in a case, and lately, it seemed he was always working.

Derek jerked his head. "Shall we?"

Jackson nodded and followed his former mentor. A line of crime scene tape crossed the path. He gave his name and displayed the ranger badge pinned to his shirt before slipping underneath the bright yellow barrier.

Derek waited until Jackson caught up with him. "One female victim. Caucasian. Single gunshot wound. The ID isn't official—the coroner will do that with finger-prints—but I recognized her. Elena Harris. Local. She attends community college at night and works full time for The Kingston Law Firm as a receptionist."

Interesting. Kingston Law Firm was a criminal defense firm. It was owned and operated by the Kingston family. Influential and wealthy, they had connections with state senators and the governor. "Could her murder have something to do with a case the law firm was working on?"

Derek grunted in reply. "Everything is on the table at this point."

The path narrowed, following alongside the creek. Bright lights were placed periodically to light the way. The air was scented with pine. Jackson's boots sank into the damp earth. Derek deviated and shortly they were standing in a small defoliated area. A woman wearing a yellow dress lay on the forest floor. Blood stained her clothes. An exercise shirt and a towel had been used in a futile effort to staunch the wounds.

Jackson's stomach curdled. Death was never easy to look at, but this... "Pip—" He stopped himself, noting the crime scene technicians and the coroner's assistant on scene. "Detective Jensen found her?"

"Sorta. She heard some screams, went to investigate, and Elena ran out of the bushes straight toward her." Derek's tone grew grim. "Piper tried to save her, but there was nothing to be done." He gestured to some trees. "The killer came close but was scared off when he heard sirens. Cell service is terrible out here, but Piper had the sense to send me a text requesting backup. That got through."

Jackson crouched next to the victim. Long blond hair tangled with leaves. Her skin was ghostly pale. Flies were already trying to gather. They were waved off by the coroner's assistant.

Young. Far too young.

"She's dressed casually. Barefoot." He rose. "She wasn't hiking."

"No. We located her car in a parking lot on the west side of the nature preserve. I suspect she met someone here and then was lured or forced to a nearby field." His jaw tightened as he pointed to the bruises on her face. "The killer beat her before shooting her."

Jackson felt his own blood heat with anger. "Did you recover her cell phone?"

"No. Her purse is also missing. We found her shoes in the field where she was shot." Derek frowned. "Beating implies anger. It's up close and personal."

Jackson didn't want to think about the young woman's last moments. Or the agony Piper must be experiencing. She had a tough outer shell, but it hid a sensitive heart. Or it used to, anyway. It'd been ten years since they last saw each other. Jackson didn't even know Piper anymore.

He blew out a breath. "If she met someone here, that indicates it was a person she knew and felt safe with, but doesn't rule out a former client. Elena may not have appreciated how violent the person was."

"Agreed. Considering the influence the Kingston family has, this could turn into a circus. I'd like the Texas Rangers to run the investigation. My staff is overworked and most of them don't have the experience necessary to handle this kind of murder. With one exception..." Derek met Jackson's gaze. "Piper. She spent nearly five years working as a homicide detective in Bismarck. Given the history between the two of you, I didn't want to assign her to the case without speaking to you first."

"I appreciate it." Jackson didn't know how to answer. Could he work with Piper? It felt silly to say no, considering their romance had been short-lived. One summer. That was all. It'd blazed hot and fast, and ultimately, Jackson had gotten burned. "Let me speak to her first. I have to take her statement anyway. Then we can decide how to proceed."

"Understood." Derek pointed to a marked trail. "Head that way. She's at the creek."

Jackson took one last look at the victim and then squared his shoulders before following the broken foliage to the creek. Forensic techs scoured the woods for clues. Trash, discarded cigarettes, anything that might tie the killer to the crime scene would be collected. It would take time to go through it all. Investigations could be painstaking, but paying attention to details was necessary. One piece of evidence could break the whole case open.

The tree line broke and then... there she was.

Piper.

She stood next to the creek, shoulders hunched against the cold. Someone—probably Derek—had given her a jacket. It swallowed her slender frame. Her honey-colored waves were pulled back into a ponytail that highlighted the curve of her cheeks and her long neck. Mud coated her tennis shoes. There was dried blood on her hands. A golden Labrador sat patiently by her side, his leash hanging from her right wrist.

Seeing her was equivalent to a gut-punch. Jackson's breath stalled. It was shocking, and more than embarrassing, to realize his first urge was to hug her. Before they were sweethearts, they'd been friends. Now they were strangers. Maybe they always had been. After all, Piper had dropped him. Packed up and left town, leaving behind a note with very little explanation.

We weren't meant to be. I'm sorry.

Piper always had been tougher than steel. People had warned him of that. Jackson hadn't listened and had gotten his heart broken for the trouble. Problem was, he couldn't even be angry with her about it. How could Jackson possibly blame her for packing up and leaving town after being assaulted? He'd always understood her desire for a fresh start. What hurt was that she left him behind.

Just like his mother had.

"Hi, Jackson." She jutted up her chin, her gaze guarded. "It's been a long time."

"It has. I didn't know you moved back to town."

He'd been out of the loop since his granddad died five years ago. Jackson still had friends in town, but as with Derek, didn't speak with them often. Before tonight, he'd thought Piper was still living in North Dakota.

The lab greeted him with some sniffs. Jackson rubbed the dog's ears. "Who's this?"

"Moxie. He belongs to my sister..." She sighed. "It's a

long story." Piper met his gaze. "I want to work together on this case, Jackson. Things between us..."

"That was a long time ago." He didn't want to get into it any more than she did.

"Perhaps, but there's history, and not all of it is good." Piper sucked in a deep breath and let it out slowly. "You have no reason to give me a chance, but I'm asking. Please. I have experience and I'm a good investigator."

A rattle came from behind them. Jackson turned to see the coroner and her assistant lift a black body bag holding the victim onto a waiting gurney. They struggled to transport it down the narrow pathway. A wheel screeched, like nails on a chalkboard.

Piper's expression hardened, gaze locked on the gurney. "Her blood is on my hands. I was with Elena when she took her last breath. Whoever did this... I want to lock him up and throw away the key forever." She turned back to face Jackson. "Will you let me help you?"

THREE

Piper hated to feel like she was begging for anything, but in this instance, she'd swallow her pride. For Elena. She deserved justice, and whoever had murdered the young woman was a vicious predator. He needed to be taken off the streets. Piper wasn't good at much, but she was an excellent detective. Passionate. Dedicated. Persistent. She poured her heart into her job and took pride in standing up for those who couldn't—either because they were too scared to or, as in Elena's case, had been silenced.

Jackson was quiet for a long moment. His expression carefully hid whatever he was thinking, but Piper knew him well enough to guess. He didn't want to work with her. Irritation flared. Their romance was ancient history. Surely, as adults, they could put that aside and work together to catch a killer.

"Let's focus on one thing at a time," Jackson said diplomatically. "I need your statement."

A stall tactic. It wasn't a yes, but it also wasn't a no. She'd take it.

Jackson pulled a notepad from the inside pocket of his blazer. Time had chiseled his features, sharpening his jaw line and deepening the cleft in his chin. His mother's Italian heritage was evident in the tawny color of his skin and prominent cheekbones. The slope of his nose was slightly crooked. That was new. As was the faint scar along the curve of his upper lip. His hair was the color of rich walnut, left slightly long on top, and styled in its natural curls.

A lock fell across his forehead. Piper had the insane urge to brush it back. Instead, she tightened her hold on Moxie's leash and shifted her feet.

"Take me through what happened from the beginning."

Jackson's question snapped her mind into focus. Piper sucked in a breath and then explained everything that'd transpired since first hearing Elena's scream. Her words were clipped. Efficient. Flat. She'd learned long ago to lock up her emotions. "I sensed the attacker in the woods but didn't glimpse him. Sirens from approaching patrol cars scared him off. I didn't go in pursuit because Elena needed first aid."

Sympathy shone in Jackson's expression. "You did the right thing."

Had she? Elena had died anyway, and the killer had gotten away. Would've, could've, should've. Her life was full of them. Piper shoved the thought aside. "Have you been to the field where she was beaten and shot?"

"Not yet."

"Come on. I'll take you."

She led him to a deer trail. It was narrow, and she let Moxie surge in front. His tail bobbed in the flashlight beam from her cell phone. Branches tugged at her clothing and hair. Piper didn't want to think about how she must look. Sweaty from her run, blood on her hands, messy hair and dirty clothing. It was a silly and vain train of thought, considering a woman had lost her life tonight, but seeing Jackson highlighted all her old insecurities. He was strikingly handsome. And she was so... plain.

"How often do you run along the creek?" Jackson asked, his voice carrying on the light wind.

"Every Wednesday. It's my only free evening." Piper waved away a mosquito. "My sister had a car accident about seven months ago. Broke her knee and shattered her pelvis. She's doing better, but the recovery has been slow. I moved home to help take care of the kids. Finn is eight. Emma is five. As you can imagine, the kids, along with my job as a detective, keep me busy. I don't have as much time for myself these days."

"I suppose not. What about Ava's husband?"

"They're divorced."

"I'm sorry to hear that."

Piper's nose wrinkled. "It's for the better. Rob is useless and did nothing except bring my sister down." She stepped over a large tree root. "Ava moved back to Rock Fort after her divorce to live closer to Grandma Mary a few years ago."

Grandma Mary wasn't biologically related to them,

but was family all the same. She'd been their foster mother. Whenever Piper and her sister were removed from their mother's home, it was Grandma Mary who took them in. They'd bounced between her home and their mother's for most of their childhoods. She'd been the stable adult in their lives.

"Anyway, Ava is doing much better since the accident, but the doctors don't want her to overdo it. She still hasn't been cleared to drive and does physical therapy three times a week."

"I imagine it's a full-time job keeping Ava off her feet."

Piper laughed. "You know my sister well. She's as stubborn as they come."

Her tone was full of affection. Ava and Piper were incredibly close and loved each other deeply. They'd supported each other through everything: a difficult childhood, Piper's assault, and Ava's divorce. Neither of the women had known their fathers, and with their mother unreliable in life and now deceased, they depended on each other.

"Thank goodness for Grandma Mary," Piper said. "She's a tremendous help. We couldn't have gotten through this without her, but she's in her seventies now, and it's not fair to send her all over town doing drop-offs and pickups."

"You're gonna be in trouble if I tell her what you just said."

She laughed. "I know. Don't get me wrong, Grandma Mary is spry, and I would never count her out. But these are her retirement years. She's already dedicated so much of her time to us. I want her to put her feet up without feeling guilty about it." Piper ducked under a tree branch and held it up for Jackson. "Speaking of family, how's your dad?"

"Fantastic. He moved to Hawaii shortly before I graduated from college and loves it." Jackson took the branch from her and deftly bent at the waist to avoid knocking his head. "He says the sea and the sand are good for his soul, although I think it's his new wife that really makes the difference."

"Your dad remarried?" Piper's brows arched. "That's..."

"Surprising? Yeah, I know. No one was more shocked than Dad. But Grandad had been talking to him about opening his heart and second chances and all that, so maybe it wasn't as unexpected as it seemed. His wife, Kirstina, is kind and open. I like her a lot, and more importantly, she makes Dad happy. He put his life on hold to raise me after Mom left. It's nice to see he's finally got a bit of happiness."

"I'm glad." Piper had always liked Jackson's dad. Richard was kind and empathetic. It'd been nearly everyone else in town who'd disapproved of the relationship between Jackson and Piper that'd eaten away at her. Jackson's family was wealthy and well-respected. Hers was poor and dysfunctional. It'd been an opposites-attract romance, which only worked in story books and fairy tales. In real life, it always failed.

Up ahead, light filtered onto the path. Spotlights had

been placed in the field to aid the technicians while they gathered evidence. Piper stepped free of the tree line and held tight to Moxie's leash. The field was a riot of flowers. Gorgeous bluebonnets and daffodils and pink ladies. This had once been her sanctuary as a teen. Her place to escape when the house became too loud and confrontational.

Piper gestured with her phone toward the dark blood staining the tamped-down grass a short distance away. "That's where he shot her."

"Did you hear gunshots?"

"No, but I was next to the creek, and it's possible the killer used a silencer."

Jackson studied the field for a long moment. "So, he lures her here somehow. Beats her. Shoots her. And then... what? She ran?"

"Probably. My guess is the killer thought Elena was dead. She surprised him by running off. He gave chase, but things got complicated when Elena ran into me."

A shudder rippled down her spine. Piper could envision the pain and terror Elena must've felt all too clearly. She remembered lying on the kitchen floor of her childhood home, her broken arm aching, staring up at the masked man pointing a gun at her. In the end, her life had only been spared by the unexpected arrival of her mother.

She shoved the memories aside. "I'll show you the parking lot." Piper waved to the crime scene technicians working in the area before heading down another path. This one was wider. Jackson kept pace beside her. Moxie trailed behind them now. He was getting tired. Piper could sympathize. The adrenaline had faded from her system and exhaustion was seeping into her muscles.

Jackson must've noticed because he slanted a glance in her direction. "I'm sorry. You're tired, and it's been a long night. Derek can escort me."

"No, it's fine." She wanted to work this case. The more he asked for her help, the better.

She glanced at him. In the darkness, it was hard to see his expression, but the badge pinned to his chest glimmered in the light from his phone. "How long have you been with the Rangers?"

"A few years. I started as a state trooper and waited for an opening."

"Do you like it?"

"I do. My boss, Lieutenant Rodriguez, runs a tight ship but values camaraderie. We get together as a group as much as possible and are very supportive of one another. It's like a family." His lips curved up into a smile. "A growing one. I've attended more weddings in the last three years than I have in all my life. And some of those couples have kids or are expecting. Our monthly BBQs are quickly becoming overrun with ankle biters."

Piper laughed. "It sounds nice." She grew quiet for a moment. There wasn't a wedding ring on his left hand, but that didn't mean anything. Some members of law enforcement didn't wear jewelry for safety reasons. "And what about you? Dating anyone special these days?"

"No." His tone was even, but she sensed the tension

coming from him. This was wading too close to sour feelings. "You?"

She shook her head. "Too many complications in my life." Piper tossed him a wry smile. "Between my sister, the kids, and my job, I'm barely keeping my head above water. I can't remember the last time I had a vacation. Have you visited your dad in Hawaii?"

"I went to his wedding last year. It's beautiful. Granddad..." His voice trailed off as a flash of grief creased his features. "He loved it."

Piper's heart clenched. Jackson's grandfather had helped raise him after his mother left. "I was sorry to hear of your grandfather's passing. You must miss him terribly."

"I do, but Granddad was ninety. Can't ask for much more time than that." He blew out a breath. "He left me his house. I don't have the foggiest notion what to do with it. The idea of selling it hurts too much, and with so much of my life consumed with work, it's hard to find time to properly take care of it."

"Would you ever move back?"

He shrugged. "I don't know. Maybe. Right now, it's not an option. My assigned area as a ranger is three counties over, so the commute would be rough. I'm only filling in on this case because my colleague was shot in the line of duty."

"Shot?" She inhaled. "Will he be okay?"

"Oh yeah. Cole's as tough as they come."

They exited the forest onto an asphalt parking lot. A country lane weaved its way through the woods toward the highway. Piper slapped a mosquito on her neck. She would need to bathe in calamine lotion tonight. "This parking lot isn't used often. No cameras." She gestured to the rusted sedan under a lone spotlight. "That's registered to Elena. Derek will have it towed and searched, but it's likely the killer came in his own vehicle."

The hair on the back of Piper's neck stood on end. She turned, peering into the woods. Shadows shifted in the trees as a cloud passed over the moon.

Jackson joined her. "What is it?"

"I don't know." Goosebumps peddled her skin. An owl hooted somewhere in the trees. Piper had the sense they were being watched, but... was she imagining it?

She scanned the tree line again.

Nothing stirred.

Then Moxie tugged on his leash. The scruff on his neck grew larger and he growled.

Unease roiled Piper's insides. She instinctively reached for her handgun. "I think someone's out there."

FOUR

Jackson immediately took a protective stance in front of Piper. His hand snapped to the weapon at his hip, even as his gaze scanned the tree line. Moonlight painted the leaves silver and illuminated the empty parking lot, but deeper in the woods, it was pitch black.

Moxie growled again. The Labrador clearly sensed a threat. A person? Or an animal? Jackson held his breath, straining to listen for any unusual sound. Wind rippled through the leaves. If something was out there in the woods, it wasn't moving. Goosebumps pebbled across Jackson's skin. He didn't like this. Not one bit.

"Piper, call or text for backup." Jackson kept his voice pitched low.

"It could be an animal." Piper matched his whisper. She pulled her cell from her bag. "Moxie isn't a guard dog."

"Regardless, we'll need a lift back to our vehicles." He had no intention of trekking back through the woods.

Not with a potential killer nearby. Even with backup, it would be impossible to clear the area entirely. That would take a team of men and search dogs. They didn't have the resources for that.

"Backup is on the way." Piper clicked her phone off.

A rumble came from Moxie's chest. This was deep and followed by a sharp bark. She held his leash tightly. "He's never acted like this before."

Whatever was in the woods was upsetting the dog, and that was good enough for Jackson. It was better to be safe than sorry. Right now, they were too exposed. He kept his gaze locked on the surrounding area but took Piper's elbow with his left hand. He gently tugged her backward into the protection of a large oak tree near the entrance of the parking lot. It was little help if the person in the woods had night vision goggles. He prayed that wasn't the case.

Jackson's heart beat against his rib cage. Was someone out there? Elena's killer? If so, what was he hoping to accomplish by lurking in the woods? His thoughts ping-ponged even as he kept his gaze scanning the area. There was only one reasonable explanation. Elena's killer was worried that Piper had seen something tonight. Perhaps he was hoping to catch her alone in order to remove the only potential witness.

He wouldn't succeed. Jackson would defend Piper with his life. The ranger badge pinned to his chest demanded he protect the innocent. Even if it didn't... this was Piper.

He glanced at the woman by his side. Her face was

hidden in shadows, but her posture was rigid. Like him, she held her handgun in one hand, ready to use it should the need arise. Piper was a trained law enforcement officer. She could protect herself, yet neither logic nor reason did anything to stop this intense urge to shield her from harm.

It'd always been like that. His need to protect, her need for independence. They'd never been able to find the right balance. Piper was tougher than anyone he'd ever met, but every once in a while, he'd glimpsed her vulnerability. She felt deeply even if she didn't show it. Over time, and with trust, Jackson thought he'd break through her hard shell and finally she'd fully let him in. He'd wanted Piper to rely on him to be her safe shelter. Turn to him in times of need and pain.

He'd wanted to take care of her.

She'd wanted to be free.

The rumble of an engine drew closer moments before a Rock Fort Sheriff's Department SUV entered the lot, followed by two more patrol cars. Jackson breathed a sigh of relief but didn't slip from the protective cover of the large oak tree. Instead, he called Derek over to them and explained the situation. "It may be nothing, but I didn't think it wise to take the chance."

"Smart move." Derek frowned, his gaze darting toward Piper before settling back on Jackson. Without being told, he'd already come to the same conclusion Jackson had earlier—that the killer might be targeting Piper. "We'll search the area. In the meantime, use my SUV to take Piper home."

"That's unnecessary." Piper holstered her weapon. "I can stay and help—"

"No. It's been a long night. An emotional one." Derek tossed his keys toward Jackson. "Go home, Piper. Get some rest and we'll talk again in the morning. That's an order."

She looked perturbed to be sent home but was wise enough not to argue with her boss. "My truck?"

"It's trapped behind a dozen vehicles. I'll have a deputy bring it to your house once the crime scene clears out." Derek patted Moxie on the head and then nodded toward Jackson. There was a silent message in that small gesture. An order to make sure Piper got home safely and everything was okay before he headed back to the scene.

Jackson didn't need the order, but he was glad Piper had someone who was watching out for her best interests. He also appreciated that Derek said nothing about his suspicions. There was no need to scare Piper unnecessarily. They didn't know if there was even a person in the woods. Not yet.

Hopefully, Derek and his deputies would find proof, one way or another.

FIVE

Fifteen minutes later, Jackson pulled up to the Jensen house at the end of a cul-de-sac. Light poured from the windows on the first floor. The grass was overgrown, and the bushes needed a trim, but the blue shutters had been recently painted. A bicycle lay discarded next to the front stoop.

Moxie, who'd been calmly lying in the back seat, rose to his feet and gave an excited bark.

"Someone's happy to be home." Piper popped out of the vehicle before Jackson could circle the vehicle to open her door. She released Moxie and he ran to the front stoop, tongue hanging out.

Jackson would swear the dog was smiling. His own lips lifted in a grin.

"Come inside." Piper closed the rear door of the SUV. She'd been quiet for most of the car ride, but now seemed to get a second wind. Or maybe, like Moxie, she was relieved to be home. "I made lasagna for dinner, and I'm sure there's leftovers."

His stomach growled at the mention of food. Jackson had skipped lunch and breakfast. "I don't want to intrude."

"You aren't. Grandma Mary will be perturbed if I don't invite you in. Don't sentence me to a lecture." Her lips twisted into a teasing grin. "Besides, the only thing open at this hour is Mo's Diner on the highway. I wouldn't wish that food on my worst enemy."

He laughed. Mo's was a dingy watering hole with greasy food that always made Jackson's stomach hurt. Piper's lasagna sounded much better. She'd always been an excellent cook, a side effect of practically raising herself. Besides, it might be better to hang out a bit at her house. It would give Derek time to search the woods and update Jackson. It was highly risky to come after a law enforcement officer, but Elena's murder had been brutal.

Jackson wouldn't take chances. "Dinner would be great. Thanks, Piper."

She led him inside the house. It had an open floor plan with a large living room and dining area. Music and singing came from the kitchen. Moxie ran ahead, his tail disappearing around the corner. An excited squeal followed. A little girl, if Jackson had to guess.

"I'm finally home," Piper called out. "And I've brought a guest."

Mary appeared, holding a dish towel in one hand. Her once dark hair had surrendered to the soft silver of age and lines creased her skin, deeper along the edges of her eyes and mouth. Everything about her was soft. From the pastel color of her blouse to the delicate knot holding the apron around her waist. Warmth mingled with worry as she took in Piper's disheveled appearance.

She rushed to give her surrogate daughter a hug. "I'm glad you're home safe and sound." She pulled back. "I've been praying on and off since Derek called to say there'd been an incident in the nature preserve. Are you okay?"

"I'm desperate for a shower and some food, but otherwise, I'm fine." Piper lifted her lips in a smile. "Don't worry, Grandma Mary."

"Not gonna happen, baby. It's part of the job description." Mary laughed lightly, as some of the tension drained from her shoulders. She glanced at Jackson, seeming to register his presence for the first time. His eyes widened as a broad smile creased her cheeks. "Well, now, Jackson Barker. It's been far too long since you've darkened our doorstep."

He removed his cowboy hat. "It's good to see you, ma'am. Sorry for dropping in unexpectedly."

"Nonsense. You're always welcome." She gave him a motherly hug and then backed away to stare him in the face. "My word, you're the spitting image of your granddaddy. It's uncanny." Her broad mouth split into a grin. "Did I ever tell you he was the most eligible bachelor in Rock Fort? But he only had eyes for Bessie. From the moment those two sat together in English class, it was love at first sight."

"That's exactly what Grandad used to say." Jackson had fond memories of his grandmother. She'd passed when he was in middle school and his grandfather was never the same.

"Jackson is a Texas Ranger now." Piper toed off her dirty tennis shoes. "He's helping on the case. I promised him some lasagna."

"Well, there's plenty left—"

"Aunt Piper!" A shout came from across the room. A little girl with pigtails and an impish grin appeared. She tackled Piper with an enthusiastic hug.

Piper's smile widened and she hugged the little girl with abandon before tickling her. Peals of laughter poured out. The obvious joy brought a smile to Jackson's face. He couldn't remember a time he'd ever seen Piper so content. So happy. After the scare they'd had in the woods, it was a welcome respite.

"Emma Grace, how many times do I have to tell you not to shout in the house?" Ava limped into the room. Her blonde hair, the same shade as Piper's, was pulled back into a low ponytail, but unlike her younger sister's curly locks, Ava's was pin straight. She had dark brown eyes and high cheekbones. A brace placed over her soft cotton yoga pants stretched from her right ankle to upper thigh.

The worry lines creasing her forehead eased as she greeted her baby sister. "Hi, Piper." Her brows lifted at the sight of Jackson, but if she was surprised by his presence, she was too polite to say so. "Jackson, it's been a long time. You're looking well."

"Thank you. Piper told me about your accident. I'm glad you're recovering."

"This little munchkin is Emma." Piper wriggled her fingers, causing another peal of laughter. Then she gestured to the lanky boy standing close to Ava as if worried she might fall. "And this is Finn. Kiddos, I'd like you to meet Texas Ranger Jackson Barker."

Finn stepped forward to shake Jackson's hand. The youngster resembled his mother with large dark eyes and blonde hair. "Nice to meet you, sir."

Jackson nodded, pleased by the boy's manners. "You too."

Emma eyed him up and down. "What's a Texas Ranger?"

He crouched to her level. "It's a fancy name for a police officer."

"Oh, like Aunt Piper. Except she works for the sheriff. And she's a detective. Are you a detective?"

He chuckled. "Kinda."

"Is Aunt Piper the boss of you? She's the boss of me when my mommy isn't here. Or when she's sleeping."

"Aunt Piper isn't the boss of Ranger Barker." Ava pulled Emma toward her with an apologetic look in Jackson's direction. "It's time to get ready for bed. Say goodnight, please."

There was a flurry of activity as Mary and the kids went upstairs to start the bedtime routine. Ava followed at a much slower rate, sitting on the stairs one at a time and pulling herself up backward. Moxie followed, his tail wagging wildly, as he repeatedly kissed Ava's cheek.

Jackson toed off his boots to avoid tracking dirt on to the faded carpet. "Nice kids."

"They are." Piper grinned. "Sorry about Emma. Her favorite game is twenty questions." She gestured to a door near the staircase. "There's a small bathroom, if you'd like to wash up for dinner. Give me fifteen minutes and I'll meet you in the kitchen."

"Take your time."

Jackson dipped inside the tiny room and scrubbed his hands. His chin bore thick whiskers and his shirt was rumpled after tramping through the woods. He needed a shower, but that would have to wait. Probably for hours. The investigation into Elena's murder was just getting started, and after dinner, he'd return to the crime scene.

Distressed cabinets, dated appliances, and a small kitchen nook gave the space a homey feel. A picture window overlooked the backyard. The scent of warm pasta and tomato sauce caused his stomach to growl. The sounds of footsteps overhead indicated Ava and kids were moving around on the upper floor.

A moment later, Piper joined him. She must've taken a quick shower before changing into a soft pair of yoga pants and a T-shirt. Her hair was dry—she hadn't washed it—but the blood was gone from her hands and arms.

"Sorry about the noise. Sounds like a herd of elephants." Piper raised her gaze to the ceiling. "It's mostly Moxie. And Emma. If only I had the same level of energy they did." She shook her head affectionately before glancing at Jackson. "What can I get you to drink? There's soda and water. Or I can make a fresh pot of coffee."

"Water is fine for now. Is there anything I can do to help?"

"Nope, it's all ready. Have a seat."

He settled in a chair and watched her bustle around the kitchen. It was strange to be with Piper. Unsettling and yet familiar too. Her movements were graceful and efficient. She'd been through an ordeal tonight, but looking at her now, no one would know. Piper had always been good at compartmentalizing her emotions. Clearly that hadn't changed in the last ten years.

"Here you go." Piper set a plate on the table in front of him. It was piled high with lasagna, a side salad, and fresh garlic bread. She'd fixed a smaller plate for herself. Within moments, she had silverware and glasses filled with water on the table too.

Once everything was ready and Piper was seated, she met his gaze. "Why don't you lead us in grace?"

Jackson nodded and then bowed his head. "Lord, we thank you for the food we are about to receive. May it nourish our bodies. We also ask that you watch over the investigators as they gather evidence, and we pray for Elena's family. May You be with them in their heartache. Amen."

"Amen." Piper's eyes uncharacteristically shimmered with tears. Derek was right. The incident in the woods had shaken her more than she would admit. For good reason. Elena had died in her arms.

Jackson couldn't stand it. He placed a hand over hers. "I'm sorry, Piper. I meant what I said earlier. You did all you could."

She squeezed his hand and then pulled away to take a sip of water. Her gaze avoided his. Jackson didn't know what he'd hoped her response would be, but discussing emotionally charged topics had never been her forte. Anything that couldn't be changed went into a vault.

They discussed lighthearted things for the rest of the meal. The weather, Emma's new artwork hanging on the fridge, and Jackson's vacation to Hawaii. Eventually, the quiet settled over them, punctuated only by the scrape of the fork against their plates. The footsteps upstairs stilled. As Jackson's stomach filled, his energy returned. He'd been hungrier than he realized, and the lasagna was the perfect dinner after a long day. "You outdid yourself, Piper. The food is amazing."

"Thanks." She cleared her throat and then took a drink of water. Fiddled with her napkin. "Truth is, it was a way to get a quiet moment with you away from the scene." She took a deep breath and raised her gaze to meet his. "I owe you an apology, Jackson. For leaving like I did."

He pushed away his empty plate. "It was a long time ago, Piper. You were hurting. I understood."

The trouble was, he did. Piper never had it easy. Her childhood was spent bouncing between her mentally ill and drug-addicted mother's house and Grandma Mary. She'd endured nasty gossip from some of the less well-meaning townsfolk. Through it all, she held her head high and fought to be respected.

The assault shattered her. Her feisty and determined nature had been subdued. She'd jumped at her own shadow and suffered through fresh whispered gossip from neighbors. So no, Jackson didn't blame her one bit for fleeing a town that held such terrible memories for her.

What really hurt was that she never asked him to go with her.

He would have. In a heartbeat. Yes, they'd been ridiculously young, but he'd envisioned dating throughout college. Marriage. Supporting each other's careers and, eventually, children. The way Piper left... breaking up with him in a *letter*... it'd punched a hole in his heart. And maybe that was the crux of the entire problem. He'd loved Piper more than she had him.

All of that was ancient history. Jackson had forgiven her a long time ago, and there was no need to rehash their mistakes. "I appreciate the apology, but it's unnecessary. There are no hard feelings on my part."

Her shoulders sagged. "I'm glad. It's bothered me..."

"No need to let it trouble you one bit further."

His cell phone beeped with an incoming text, interrupting their conversation. He scanned the message from Derek. "There were no signs of footprints in the woods near the parking lot. No indication that anyone was hiding in the trees."

Piper relaxed against the kitchen chair with a sigh. "Moxie must've just caught the scent of an animal."

Jackson nodded, relief unfurling inside him. Piper wasn't in any danger. He rose from his chair. He'd been away from the crime scene for too long. "I should go. Thank you for dinner."

"It was nothing." Piper followed him to the door. She chewed on her bottom lip. "I meant what I said earlier. I'd like to be involved in the investigation."

Jackson settled his cowboy hat on his head. A small part of him wondered if Piper had offered the apology to wriggle her way back into his good graces, but he quickly quashed the notion. She was many things, but manipulative wasn't one of them. No, he'd seen how upset she was at the crime scene and then again during the prayer.

How could he deny her the opportunity to catch Elena's killer? They were both adults. Professionals. Whatever feelings might arise while working together, he'd handle it.

He shrugged on his jacket. "I'd be happy to have your assistance, Piper. Let's convene tomorrow morning to discuss what we know so far and who we should interview first."

Warmth filled her expression, drawing attention to her eyes. They were deep blue. Almost purple. The color of bluebonnets at the height of their flowering season. Faint lines branched out from the corners, delicate and distracting. Jackson tore his gaze away to open the front door. "See you tomorrow."

She stopped him with a hand on his arm. Heaven help him, he felt the heat of her palm straight through his jacket.

"Thank you, Jackson. It means a lot."

Oh man. The appreciation in her expression twisted his insides in funny ways. Jackson nodded, not trusting his voice, and then fled into the cool night air. He waited on the porch for the lock to snick into place. He sensed Piper was standing on the other side of the door. Several feet and a plane of wood were all that separated them.

That and a pile of hurt. Misunderstandings. Heartache.

Jackson took a deep breath. He'd made mistakes over the years. Had regrets. But this... a tiny voice in the back of his mind whispered this might well be the worst of them all. Working with Piper would test every one of the walls around his heart.

He prayed they'd stay intact.

SIX

He was coming for her.

Piper ran. Her feet pounded against the dirt. Tree branches clawed at her clothes. Her heart raced. She couldn't escape. The fear was encompassing. It tasted bitter on her tongue. Panic trapped the scream in her throat as a large form suddenly appeared in front of her.

Arms encircled her. They sucked the last of the air from her lungs as she tumbled to the forest floor. She fought, clawing against the man holding her down as the surrounding images shifted. The kitchen in her mother's trailer appeared. Chipped linoleum flooring. The groceries she'd brought over scattered all around. Oppressive summer heat making it hard to breathe. Sweat poured down her back as she stared up at the masked man hovering over her. His eyes were black holes. Evil intentions poured off him.

Trapped. He had her trapped.

Piper woke with a scream on her lips. The bedsheets

were tangled around her feet. She kicked them off, her breath coming in pants. Bile rose in the back of her throat, and she stumbled to the bathroom. She threw up. Tears pricked her eyes as she rested her head against the cool porcelain seat, trying her best to gather her wits and calm the sheer panic running through her body. It'd been years since she had a nightmare that fierce. She didn't need to call her old therapist to ask why. Elena's murder had triggered Piper's memories.

God, why did Elena have to die? Sometimes I can't make sense of this world or the things that happen.

Tears pricked her eyes. She let out her grief and her anger, pouring it onto God, because He was the only one strong enough to take it. Then, once she was depleted, Piper rose from the bathroom floor. She splashed cold water on her face. A quick glance at the clock confirmed there wasn't enough time to go back to bed. Instead, she brushed her teeth, took a shower, and dressed for the day.

As she was applying concealer to the hollows under her eyes, Emma appeared in the bathroom doorway. She was still dressed in her pajamas, her eyes sleepy, and her long hair tangled. In one small hand, she carried a brush.

Piper turned to face her. "Good morning, sweetheart. You're up bright and early."

"I used the alarm you gave me. Can you braid my hair?"

"Of course, I can." She pulled out the chair from under the vanity and patted it. "Come here. One braid or two?"

"One."

Emma promptly sat down and Piper went to work untangling the curls that'd worked themselves into knots. "Did you sleep well?"

"Yes." She rubbed her right eye with a balled fist. "Robbie was mean to Carolyn at the playground yesterday. He pulled her hair. She started crying. So then I told him to stop it and he called me a bad name." She met Piper's gaze in the mirror. Her youthful cheeks and sweet, round face offset the seriousness in her expression. "I explained everything to Mrs. Hutchinson. She gave Robbie a talking to. Pulling hair and calling people names is against the rules."

Mrs. Hutchinson was Emma's teacher. The older woman was compassionate, but she didn't let the kids get away with anything unacceptable. Piper liked her a great deal.

"Great job, Emma. You handled that exactly as you were supposed to." Piper weaved the light-colored strands of her niece's hair into a tight braid before wrapping the end with an elastic band. "I'm proud of you for sticking up for your friend."

Her niece had a heart of gold and was a fearless champion of any underdog. Ava said Emma was exactly like Piper. She appreciated the compliment, although Piper believed Emma was a much better version. She wasn't jaded. She was full of joy and light and everything good in the world.

Emma bloomed under Piper's praise. A broad smile stretched across her face. Then she admired the braid in the mirror. "That looks good." She gave her a fierce hug. "Thanks, Aunt Piper."

"You're welcome." Warmth infused her insides. Piper held on to Emma for a second or two more. "Go get dressed and come down for breakfast. I don't want you to be late for school."

"Okay." She skipped out of the bathroom.

Emma's happiness brought a smile to Piper's face and erased the last of the darkness caused by her nightmare. She hurried downstairs. The scent of coffee and bacon greeted her. Ava stood at the stove in her robe, the brace on her leg already attached over the leg of her pajamas. Several surgeries had put her sister back together after the car accident, and while she'd come a long way, things were far from 100 percent. She would probably need one more surgery at the end of the summer and was currently undergoing physical therapy.

Piper waved her sister from the stove. "Let me do it. Sit down."

"I'm fine." Ava stubbornly blocked the pan of eggs and held on to the spatula. "It's easier for me in the morning when I'm well-rested. I did my stretches already and the physical therapist said it's good for me to be standing." She eyed Piper, her gaze lingering on the dark circles concealer did little to cover. "You didn't sleep well."

"Nightmares." Piper poured a cup of coffee and then refilled Ava's. The rich, dark brew smelled heavenly. She drank some and popped bread in the toaster. "Finn outside with Moxie?"

"Yep." Ava kept stirring the eggs. "Want to talk about it?"

"The nightmare? No."

"What about working with Jackson?"

"Not that either."

"Nice try, kid, but you aren't getting out of both those topics. I'll pick the safer of the two." Ava's brows arched. "You and Jackson haven't seen each other in years and then you invite him home for dinner. Granted, it's been a while since I've been on the dating scene, but I know what attraction looks like and you two still have it."

Piper groaned. Despite her failed marriage, Ava was a romantic. She needed to nip this in the bud. "First of all, Jackson and I are working together on a *murder* case. There's nothing fun about that. Second, I invited him in for dinner because it was the polite thing to do."

"Did you apologize for breaking up with him in a letter?"

She slid some more bread into the toaster. "If you must know, yes, I did. He said it was water under the bridge. No hard feelings."

Ava was quiet for a long moment. Piper glanced at her sister, recognizing the furrowed brow and the way Ava was intensely stirring the scrambled eggs. Her sister knew something and was debating saying it.

She narrowed her gaze. "What?"

"Grandma Mary swore me to secrecy, but now that you and Jackson are working together, I think it's better if you know." She turned to face Piper. "After you left town, for almost a year, he checked in with Grandma Mary to see how you were doing. He was devastated by the breakup. Worried about how you were after the attack... Jackson really loved you."

Dumbfounded, Piper stared at her sister. "Why didn't either of you tell me?"

"I tried. I told you to call him."

"That's not the same thing."

"No, but your letter specifically asked him not to contact you. Jackson wanted to be respectful of your wishes, but also wanted to make sure you were okay. Grandma Mary said that once you were settled in North Dakota, he stopped asking."

She sagged against the counter. "My PTSD was under control by then."

"That's what she told him." Ava turned off the burner and wiped her hands on a dish towel. "Listen, Piper, you rarely listen to me, and perhaps I'm not the best person to give advice in the romance department considering my disastrous divorce, but I wouldn't be doing my job as your big sister if I don't say this. Jackson was one of the good ones. If friendship is all there is between the two of you, then fine. Leave it there. But if you decide at some point you want more... I'd tell him." She smiled. "It's rare to get a second chance with a first love."

The back door opened, saving Piper from a response. She needed time to process everything Ava had shared.

Moxie burst into the kitchen, a ball clutched in his

mouth. Finn followed. The eight-year-old was tall for his age. He nearly came up to Piper's shoulder and was skinny as a rail. He was dressed for school in jeans and a rock band T-shirt. His hair was neatly trimmed and combed back from his face.

"Morning." Piper greeted him with a hug and a kiss on his cheek. The bread popped out of the toaster, and she placed one on Finn's plate before pouring him some juice. "Moxie is getting very good at catching your curve balls."

Finn grinned. "He sure is."

Finn washed his hands at the sink before plopping down at the table. He said a quick grace before digging into his food. Moxie collapsed at his feet. His brown eyes tracked the fork from the plate to Finn's mouth. He snuck the pup some eggs.

Ava laughed and pointed a spatula at her son. "I saw that."

Finn's grin widened. "No one wants to eat dog food after working out."

"Dogs should," she shot back.

Everyone laughed. Emma bounced into the kitchen. The next twenty minutes were spent eating breakfast and rushing through the rest of the morning routine. Grandma Mary arrived. She was driving Ava to her morning physical therapy. Finn caught the school bus. Emma shrugged on her light jacket—the morning was cool—and then her backpack. Her sparkly sneakers caught the light as she hopped down the porch steps toward Piper's SUV. Her kindergarten wasn't attached to the elementary school where Finn went. Instead, it was housed in a building near the sheriff's department, along with the preschool.

Ava waved from the doorway. "Have a great day, you two."

Piper waved back. The front door shut. Dew still coated the grass, and fluffy clouds spotted the sky. Birds chittered from the oak tree. She hit the fob on her keyring and the SUV beeped. Piper opened the door for Emma, taking the little girl's backpack so she could get seated. She glanced at the spelling sheet in her other hand. "The next word is wig."

Emma's nose wrinkled. "W."

Hair rose on the back of Piper's neck. She spun, half-expecting to see someone standing at the end of the driveway.

No one was there.

Her gaze swept the neighborhood. Sprinklers were on at the McAllisters'. Mr. Jenkins, the elderly man three doors down, weeded the area around his rose bushes. A sedan from the end of the street flashed its brake lights at the stop sign and then turned right. No one was paying Piper any mind, and nothing seemed out of the ordinary. But she couldn't shake the instinctual feeling that someone was watching her.

Real? Imaginary? Piper couldn't tell. She'd had the same sensation last night, but it'd just been an animal in the woods.

"Did you hear me, Aunt Piper?" Emma tugged on her shirt. "W-I-G. Wig."

"Correct. Great job." Piper shoved Emma's backpack in the seat next to the little girl and then closed the door. She scanned the neighborhood again.

Nothing.

Still the sense of being watched lingered.

SEVEN

A thud jolted Jackson into a sitting position.

He blinked. His eyes were blurry, and a piece of paper was stuck to his cheek. He removed it as the room came into focus. Sunshine streamed through the window, brightening the industrial-gray carpeting to a silver. The table was covered with paper. A long whiteboard with his scribbles covered one wall. His laptop sat at his elbow. He'd fallen asleep while working in a conference room at the Rock Fort Sheriff's Department.

Piper stood at the opposite side of the table. She wore black tactical pants and a knit shirt bearing the sheriff's department logo. Her blonde curls were pulled back into a neat ponytail at the base of her neck. Light makeup colored her cheeks. The scent of her perfume—something subtle that smelled faintly of orange blossoms—tickled his nose.

Jackson's heart instinctively kicked up a notch. His half-asleep brain couldn't compute much, but her beauty was striking. He, on the other hand, looked and smelled like something from a dumpster. He groaned and rubbed a hand over his scruffy chin. "What time is it?"

"Eight." Piper released the thick binder she'd dropped onto the table to wake him and then reached for a coffee resting nearby. "Here. I picked this up for you."

He accepted the offering and drank greedily. Rich caramel mixed with coffee and milk slid over his taste buds. She remembered his favorite drink. It was a tiny detail, but one that sent a wave of warmth through him. Memories he'd locked away burst free. Laughing while they taught a group of campers to fish on the lake, long talks in front of the firepit, sweet kisses that sent his heart racing. Piper had been his first love.

She sipped from her own cup, her gaze scanning the whiteboard. "Any updates on the case?"

"Yep." Jackson reached for an evidence bag lying on the conference table. "This necklace was found in the grass near the field. It must've broken when Elena fled from her killer. Look at the photo inside the locket."

Piper set her coffee down. The heart-shaped pendant inside was opened, the picture attached visible through the clear plastic bag. She inhaled sharply. "That's Elena... and Shawn Kingston." Her gaze shot up. "They were romantically involved?"

"Certainly appears that way."

The photograph was small, but Jackson had it blown up so the image was more clear. He pulled it out to show Piper. Elena, her hair styled in big curls, was kneeling behind Shawn, her arms wrapped around him.

She was kissing his cheek. Shawn covered one of Elena's hands with his own. His smile was wide, and it appeared from the angle of the picture that he'd taken the photograph. Probably with his cell phone. Or maybe with Elena's, since the picture was inside her locket.

Piper blinked. "Shawn is married."

"Yes."

The coffee suddenly tasted sour in his mouth. Shawn also had two kids. Little ones. His social media was full of happy moments and loving family photographs.

This was a complication Jackson couldn't have anticipated. He and Shawn were childhood friends. Their grandfathers had been close. Jackson had fond memories of playing together during family BBQs, fishing at the lake with Granddad, and riding horses. They'd drifted apart since high school, but still kept in touch for major life events. Jackson had attended Shawn's wedding and sent presents when his kids were born. Shawn had attended Grandad's funeral.

Elena had been brutally murdered. It was hard to imagine Shawn was responsible. Yes, he could be arrogant and entitled, reckless and a bit rebellious. But a cold-blooded killer? It didn't fit with what Jackson knew about his friend. Regardless, he had to follow the evidence.

Jackson set his coffee down and scrubbed a hand over his face. His eyes felt like there was sandpaper trapped behind the lids. "We need to be careful. We can't assume anything from one photograph. There may be an innocent explanation. Or maybe Shawn and his wife have an understanding. Not everyone has a conventional marriage."

"I suppose. What about Elena's cell phone? Or her computer? If she and Shawn were in a relationship, there should be an electronic trail. Phone calls, text messages, and more photos."

"Her cell phone hasn't been recovered and she didn't have a computer. I've already provided a warrant to her cell phone provider asking for everything they have, but it'll take them a day or two to get back to me. In the meantime, it would be helpful to access the data Elena stored in the cloud, but I need a password for that. We don't have it."

Piper studied the notes on the whiteboard and then turned to face him. "Do you plan on questioning Shawn?"

"I've been mulling that over. Shawn is a criminal defense attorney. If he was having an affair with Elena, once we show him the picture, he'll likely stop cooperating with the investigation and start doing damage control. That could compromise things."

The Kingstons were influential members of the community. Townsfolk might be unwilling to provide information to avoid being ostracized.

"On the other hand, I'm not sure how long news of this locket—and the photo—will stay contained." Jackson leaned against the table and took another sip of his coffee. "Derek runs a tight ship, but gossip runs rampant in Rock Fort. It's only a matter of time before this information leaks. I'd like to get Shawn's unfiltered response. What do you think?"

She pondered the question for a moment. "I think we should question him now. Elena worked for the Kingstons. Shawn was her boss. It makes sense to speak to him as a matter of course. He'll be expecting that. Based on his responses, you can decide whether to confront him about the photograph in the locket."

Jackson nodded. "That's a good plan. Is Derek in his office? I'll run it by him before we head out. If Shawn walks away from our interview worried about what we may uncover, he'll go on the attack. Derek will be in the first line of fire. I don't want him to be blindsided."

"He's there."

"Good. I've rented a room at the B&B across the street. Give me twenty minutes to talk to Derek, get cleaned up, and shove some breakfast in my mouth. Then we'll hit the road."

Her lips curved into a heartbreaking smile. "Thank goodness. I was worried you were going to go like that. Although I do like the cowlick."

He snorted and self-consciously ran a hand over the back of his hair. "I need a haircut."

"We can make a stop between interviews to take care of that." She waved a hand. "Go. I'm clocking you. Twenty minutes."

He laughed. Piper knew he had something of a competitive streak. He'd do what was necessary to beat the clock.

Jackson headed for the door and then glanced over

his shoulder. Piper was leaning over the paperwork, reading. Slinky strands of her hair had fallen over one shoulder. Jackson tried not to notice how the light played across the curve of her cheek.

Movement beyond her caught his attention. A man with long hair and wearing dirty clothing meandered on the sidewalk. He was talking to himself. Muttering. Coming closer to the window. Could he see inside? Jackson wasn't sure. The windows in most city office buildings were tinted for privacy, but in small rural towns, it wasn't common to do so.

Suddenly the man's eyes widened. His focus seemed to be on Piper. Her back was still turned away from the window. She glanced up, and must've seen the confusion on Jackson's face, because her head tilted. "What is it?"

Jackson opened his mouth to respond, but his heart leaped into his throat, stealing the words as the man outside pulled a gun from his pocket.

He pointed it straight at Piper.

EIGHT

"Gun!"

Instinctively, Piper's body moved before her brain fully registered Jackson's warning. She hit the floor in a heap as glass shattered behind her. A thud slammed into the back of her chair. She gasped, realizing the bullet would've hit her if she'd delayed moving. Shouting from inside the sheriff's department was followed by more gunfire.

Training and self-preservation took over as Piper belly-crawled away from the shooter. Bullets slammed into the wall on the opposite side of the conference room. Like her, Jackson was on the floor. He held his firearm in one hand, but under a barrage of gunfire, there was no chance to use it. Nor was there any real protection. The tables were too heavy to tilt and the chairs were far too small to hide anyone effectively.

The barely leashed worry etched on Jackson's face

squeezed her chest tight as they took cover in the corner of the room. He scanned her quickly. "You hit?"

"No." She pulled her own firearm. "You?"

"No."

Shouts came from outside but were too far away to make out the words clearly. "How many?"

"One shooter." Jackson raised his head and then ducked back down. "Deputies have him surrounded. We just have to hang tight while they secure him."

She gave a sharp nod. Adrenaline pulsed through her veins, heightening her senses. Although her focus was on the shattered window and the threat outside on the side-walk, she was all too aware of Jackson. Their bodies were pressed against one another, shoulder to shoulder, hip to hip. Partners. Working together to help one another.

Footsteps whispered on the sidewalk beyond the large window. Piper's pulse jumped. She adjusted the hold on her gun and held her breath.

"Piper? Jackson?"

Derek. She breathed out a sigh of relief. "We're here."

"It's clear." Derek stepped through the broken window, glass crunching under his boots. Concern furrowed his brow. "Either of you hit? Need an ambulance?"

"We're okay." Jackson rose from the floor and held out a hand for Piper.

She slid her palm into his. His grip was gentle, his skin warm. A lightning bolt of attraction shot through her, intensified by the near-death experience she'd just been through. Her pulse jumped yet again. It beat against her ribs so hard she feared Jackson could hear it.

Derek shouted orders to his deputies outside. Piper barely registered them. She was on her feet, knew she should release Jackson's hand, but couldn't bring herself to do it. Their gazes met. Held. The sea-green of his eyes captivated her. It struck Piper in that moment just how much she'd missed him. His steady presence, his protection. His friendship.

Jackson cleared his throat and released her hand, stepping away. His gaze skittered from hers.

Embarrassment heated her cheeks. What was she doing? Piper mentally berated herself for letting the moment get the best of her. At one time, Jackson might have loved her, but that was all over. She'd walked away from him. From them. Self-preservation demanded it, but she'd hurt him all the same.

There was no turning back, and Piper had no right to make their working relationship uncomfortable.

She turned toward the broken window. Deputies crowded the sidewalk. Piper strained to see through the press of bodies, but it was impossible. "What happened? Who is the shooter?"

"I didn't recognize him." Jackson bent and retrieved his cowboy hat from the floor. His jaw tightened. "But whoever he was, he aimed straight for you."

Piper reared back. "Me?" She remembered the bullet hitting the back of the chair she'd been sitting in. Her gaze shot once again to the mass of deputies. The crowd parted, and the shooter came into view. She gasped. "That's Marcus Reed."

"You know him?"

She nodded. "He lives in my old neighborhood. Marcus suffers from some kind of mental illness and often self-medicates with illegal drug use." Piper crossed the room and stepped over the window's low threshold to join Derek on the sidewalk. Marcus had his hands cuffed behind his back and was alternating between muttering under his breath and shouting nonsense at the deputies. "How on earth did Marcus get a gun? No reputable dealer would sell to him with his past drug convictions."

"I don't know." Derek's expression was stony. "Marcus goes through the trash from time to time. He may have found it. Or someone gave it to him."

It made sense. Criminals discarded their guns in dozens of ways, including simply throwing them in a dumpster.

Jackson joined them. "He fired directly at Piper."

Derek frowned. "He did?"

"I doubt he realized what he was doing." Piper jutted her chin toward Marcus, who was being hauled around the corner to the main doors of the building. His clothes were riddled with holes, and it didn't look like he'd showered in a while. "Look at him. He's high and clearly not in his right mind. Marcus has no specific reason to target me."

Derek nodded. "I'll interview him to be sure. Not that I think anything he says will make sense, but..." He shrugged. "I'll try anyway."

Jackson's worried expression didn't ease. Piper tilted her head. "What are you thinking?"

He breathed out. "I don't know." He rubbed the back of his neck. "It's weird that yesterday you interrupted a murder and then today you were nearly shot. I suppose it could be a coincidence... but it's a strange one."

It was one of the many reasons a relationship with Jackson would never work out. She couldn't drag him into all of her problems. It wasn't fair. She would do well to remember that next time sentimentality and raw emotion attempted to overtake her better judgment.

Derek was quiet, his gaze sweeping across the wrecked conference room and then lingered on the chair with the bullet lodged in the back of it. Piper knew that look well. Her boss was considering Jackson's observation, taking it in and weighing it against the evidence. From the creased furrow of his brow, he was concerned. "I agree with Jackson. It's a weird coincidence. There could be nothing to it, but I want y'all to use extra care when working the murder case."

Piper eyed the two men. "Seriously? Marcus couldn't have killed Elena. He doesn't have the ability to plan such a well-executed murder."

"I agree with that." Jackson nodded.

"So what are you suggesting? That Elena's killer gave a gun to Marcus and convinced him to shoot me? That's... farfetched. Besides, what's the point? I didn't see anything on the night Elena was killed."

His mouth flattened into a thin line. "The killer doesn't know that."

NINE

Hours later, Jackson waited in the expansive lobby of the Kingston Law Firm. His heart rate had finally settled after this morning's shooting, but the worries ping-ponging in his mind wouldn't be silent. Was the incident today connected to Elena's murder?

The thought iced Jackson's blood. He couldn't erase the image of Marcus standing outside the window on the sidewalk. The man had been looking for someone, and the moment he saw Piper, he pulled his gun.

He'd fired right at her.

"You okay over there, Barker?" Piper casually flipped through a legal magazine. She'd cleaned the glass from her hair and braided it, but a few stubborn strands had wriggled free to frame her gorgeous face. "You're awfully broody. I can practically hear the wheels in your head turning."

Jackson realized his muscles were stiff and his posture rigid. He forced his spine to relax, even as a flash of irritation bolted through him. "We're on a last name basis now?"

She didn't bother to glance away from the magazine. "Why not? I refer to most of my colleagues by their last name."

Distance. Piper was putting distance between them. Reducing their relationship to a professional one. Wasn't that what he wanted? Considering the brief moment they'd shared after the shooting stopped, Jackson should be relieved. Ten years hadn't done anything to tamp down the attraction arching between them. If anything, being around each other constantly made it worse, which is exactly what he'd been afraid of.

So yes, he should be thankful she was reinforcing the wall between them, but for some inexplicable reason, Jackson's irritation grew. They were a whole lot more than colleagues. They'd shared passionate kisses and long talks. He'd danced with her at senior prom. After her assault, he'd held her hand in the hospital all night, watching over her while she slept. There was an ocean of history between them, and what Jackson felt for Piper went far beyond the professional.

The shooting this morning had driven that point home. Those desperate seconds right after Marcus fired, Jackson hadn't known if Piper was alive or dead, and he'd been unable to think of anything else. Not even his own safety.

He still cared about her. So much more than he wanted to admit. And she was calling him by his last name.

Jackson clamped his lips together to keep from saying something that might reveal his true feelings.

Piper annoyingly kept flipping through the magazine. "You're brooding again."

"I'm fine, *Jensen*. Don't worry about it."

The words came out sharper than he'd intended, but it was too late for Jackson to take them back.

Piper's gaze shot up to meet his. She frowned. "Are you angry with me?"

He breathed out. "No. Sorry. I'm just on edge." He flexed his fingers and rolled his shoulders. "It's not every day I get shot at."

Her mouth quirked up. "Thank God for that."

Heels tapping against the lobby floor interrupted their conversation. A beautiful young woman dressed in an elegant pantsuit approached. "Ranger Barker, Detective Jensen, please follow me. Mr. Kingston can see you now."

Shawn had a corner office on the second floor of the building. It was decorated in dark woods and leather. Windows stretched along the back wall, giving a beautiful view of the nature preserve. Jackson's boots sank into plush carpeting as he crossed the room to shake his old friend's hand.

"It's so good to see you." Shawn's smile was warm. He was dressed for court in a gray suit and black tie. Time had worn lines along his forehead and created creases along the edges of his eyes, but his hair was thick and he maintained the same athletic build from high school. "How's your dad?"

"Well, thanks."

Shawn turned his attention to Piper. His smile dimmed and his handshake was less personable. Clearly there was still no love lost between Piper and Shawn. They'd never liked each other much. For good reason. Shawn was a touch arrogant and entitled. Since Piper grew up poor and with a troubled childhood, she didn't register in his world. At least... that's how Shawn wanted it to be. Jackson had always suspected his friend had a crush on Piper, but when it was unrequited, that attraction turned sour.

Shawn never handled being rejected well. It'd really caused an issue when Jackson started dating Piper. Competition between them had developed in high school, fueled by Shawn's incessant need to be better than everyone else.

Jackson had always found those aspects of Shawn's personality infuriating. Truth be told, it'd created a wedge between them as they grew older. But he also understood that Shawn was a product of his own family. Paul Kingston was charming and charismatic, but there was undercurrent of self-importance to his personality that was as natural as breathing. The Kingstons got what they wanted, and if it wasn't handed to them, then they fought for it.

Shawn gestured to a small sitting area with leather couches and a bookshelf filled with law books. "Please have a seat. My secretary said you're here to discuss Elena Harris's murder. How can I help?"

Jackson claimed the chair catercorner to Shawn. He

didn't want this to feel like an interrogation. More like a conversation. He pulled out his cell phone. "Before we get started, I'm going to record this conversation, if that's all right. It helps when I write up the report later."

"Actually, I do mind." Shawn's tone was pleasant, but there was a warning look in his eye. "This meeting is voluntary. I want to do everything possible to aid in the investigation, but there's no need to record it. I don't have much to say anyway."

A warning bell sounded in Jackson's head, but he pushed it aside. Shawn was a defense attorney. It'd been a long shot that he'd acquiesce to the recording. "How well did you know Elena?"

"Not well. She worked as a receptionist downstairs, so I would see her occasionally. We'd say hi, but that was the extent of our interaction. She seemed very nice." His expression was appropriately somber, but something about it felt manufactured, as if there was a well of emotions hiding underneath. "I was saddened to learn of her death."

Jackson nodded as if he was getting the answers he expected. "So you've never met up with Elena outside of work?"

A flicker of something flashed across Shawn's face. "Of course not." He paused, as if calculating whether Jackson might know something. "Of course, we have the occasional office party. There's an annual Christmas bash and a summer BBQ with all of our employees and their families. Last year, we took everyone to a water park in Houston. All of those take place outside of the office."

"Of course. I'm glad you mentioned those events. Did Elena ever bring a boyfriend with her?"

Shawn blinked. "Not to my knowledge."

"Do you know if she was dating anyone?"

His gaze dropped from Jackson's and he busied himself by adjusting his tie. "I wouldn't know anything about her dating life. As I said, we only knew each other professionally. It sounds cold, but I barely spoke to Elena. There was no reason for us to interact much. The receptionists are managed by our office manager. She handles the evaluations, the hiring and firing. It's my understanding you already spoke with Nancy."

"We did."

Jackson and Piper had interviewed her while waiting for Shawn to get back from court. The older woman was distraught. She cried through most of the conversation, praising Elena's work ethic and her kind disposition. Unfortunately, she hadn't known much about her personal life. Nor did she know the password to Elena's storage cloud.

"Do you know if Elena had issues with anyone? Another employee? Or maybe a client?"

Shawn fidgeted with his cuff links as he shifted on the couch. "I can't think of anyone who'd want to hurt her."

Jackson didn't miss the careful way his friend worded the answer. Neither did Piper, judging from the way her gaze narrowed slightly.

She learned forward. "But she did have an issue with someone."

"I didn't say that."

"Do you know Marcus Reed?" Jackson asked.

The quick shift in questioning gave Shawn pause. His gaze skipped between Jackson and Piper, and he fidgeted with his tie again. Buying time? Maybe. If the Kingstons had represented Marcus, it was a matter of public record. Shawn must've come to the same conclusions because he frowned. "We've represented him in the past. Pro bono. Why? Is Marcus connected to Elena's murder?"

"We're following up on all leads. Do you know if Elena ever had an issue with Marcus?"

He shrugged. "I can tell you there was never an incident between them in our offices. Outside of it... I can't say. As I've pointed out several times, I didn't know Elena well." Shawn checked his watch and then rose. "I'm sorry, but I have a client meeting that I must prepare for."

Jackson wouldn't accept the brush-off that easily. He remained seated. "I have a few more questions. I promise it won't take up much of your time."

For a moment, he thought Shawn would argue, but then he sat back down on the couch. He gave Jackson a tight smile. "Anything for an old friend."

The subtle reminder didn't escape Jackson. A warning? Perhaps. Shawn was growing increasingly agitated. He couldn't sit still, and although he seemed appropriately saddened about Elena's death, there was an underlying tension to his answers. Jackson had the distinct impression his friend was lying. About his relationship with Elena? Or about something else?

It was time to find out.

Jackson opened the file folder on his lap and removed a blown-up copy of the photograph taken from Elena's locket. Shawn blanched as he placed it on the coffee table. Then his jaw tightened. "Where did you get that?"

"In a locket. Elena was wearing it when she was murdered. If you barely knew her, how do you explain this photograph?"

A muscle in Shawn's jaw twitched. "It's not what you think."

"What do I think?"

"That I was having an affair with her. I wasn't." Shawn blew out a breath. "At our last Christmas party, there was a photo booth. The old-fashioned kind that prints the pictures in a strip. Anyway, we all took turns having our photos taken. I was there with my paralegal, making silly faces. At some point, she got out and Elena got in. She kissed my cheek. It was inappropriate, which I told her immediately after the picture was taken. How it ended up in her locket, I can't explain." He shrugged. "Maybe she had a crush on me. She wouldn't be the first woman."

Piper hummed in disbelief. "You expect us to believe that Elena had a secret crush on you? What is this, middle school?"

Shawn glowered at her. "You can believe what you want. It's the truth." He rose and strolled to his office door, opening it. "My secretary will escort you back to the lobby. If you have additional questions for our employees, please call and make an appointment ahead of time."

Piper left without a backward glance. Jackson moved more slowly. As he crossed the room, Shawn refused to meet his gaze, but the hand holding the door trembled slightly.

Jackson stopped in front of him. "Secrets have a way of getting out, Shawn. Elena is dead. There's no way to stop this investigation. I will catch her killer. If you had an affair with her and need to keep it quiet, the best way to do that is to be straightforward with me. Either way, I'm going to get to the truth."

Shawn met his gaze. The heat of his fury nearly stole Jackson's breath. "Tread lightly." He stepped forward, closing the distance between them until they were chest to chest. "My family is well respected, and townsfolk don't take kindly to rumor and innuendo. I have no intention of trying to stop your investigation, but I won't sit idly by and let you sully my good name."

The battle lines had been drawn. There was nothing more for Jackson to say. He turned and followed Piper down the hall, but the weight of Shawn's stare and the heat of his anger pursued them. It triggered every one of Jackson's alarm bells. He'd hoped this meeting would clear his friend. Instead, it put him at the top of the suspect list.

And Shawn knew it.

Outside, Jackson adjusted his cowboy hat to shield his eyes from the sun. A glance around the parking lot ensured he and Piper were alone. "What do you think?"

"He's a liar. Shawn and Elena were having an affair." She slanted a glance. "You poked a bear. You do know that, right?"

"Yeah." Jackson approached his SUV and opened the passenger side door for her. "Shawn doesn't want news about his affair spreading, which I can understand, but his reaction makes me think he has a lot more to hide. Problem is, one photograph isn't enough to prove a relationship."

"No, but women talk, especially to their friends."

He grinned. "They do?"

Piper laughed. She wasn't telling him something he didn't already know. "Shawn and Elena may have kept their relationship a secret, but I guarantee you someone in her inner circle knows. We just have to figure out who."

"Yeah. It would be good if we could find out her passcode to her cloud storage too. I don't think it was an accident the killer took her cell phone." Jackson went to close the door, but Piper stopped him.

Concern creased her features. "Shawn didn't want to admit he knew Marcus."

"No, he didn't. Honestly, it only makes me more suspicious that what happened this morning wasn't random."

She blew out a breath. "I'm not a fan of Shawn's, but he's not a fool. Hiring Marcus to shoot me is fraught with risk and complications."

"So is killing his mistress."

TEN

Jackson's words haunted Piper for the rest of the day and into the evening.

She swiped the kitchen counter with a sponge before rinsing her hands in the sink. Dinner had been a simple affair of hamburgers and salad. Piano music filtered in from the living room. Finn was practicing a new song for Sunday church service. Based on his broken starts and stops, it wasn't going well.

She sympathized. The investigation into Elena's murder wasn't going smoothly either. They'd interviewed most of Elena's friends and a few members of her extended family. Unfortunately, none of them knew anything about her dating life and no one could provide the password to her cloud storage. Piper was extremely frustrated by the lack of progress.

So far, Shawn was their strongest suspect, but they couldn't even prove he'd been having an affair with Elena.

Truth was, Piper couldn't see the pristine lawyer luring his mistress to a field, beating her, and then shooting her to death. Shawn was arrogant and he had a temper, but he wasn't the kind to get his hands dirty. Money had always been his solution to any problem. In school, he'd paid a fellow student to do his homework. Rumor had it, when he ran into legal trouble in his twenties after stealing a car from a dealership, he'd bought the vehicle at above asking price. He settled disputes with employees by increasing their severance package.

If Shawn wanted Elena's silence, he'd buy it. Worst case scenario, he'd hire someone to murder her, not actually do the killing himself.

The hum of the washing machine meant the clothes weren't ready for the dryer yet. Dishes done, and the kitchen clean, Piper had a few minutes. She settled at the table and opened her laptop. A few moments later, she accessed Elena's social media.

The young woman hadn't posted often. Maybe she'd been too busy with her college classes and work. Piper looked for pictures she was tagged in, making a list of additional friends to interview the next day. From the looks of things, Elena was well-liked, but there was seriousness to her that radiated from the images on the computer screen. It reminded Piper so much of herself...

Was that what was bothering her? The nightmare from the other night rushed back into her mind. The melding of Elena's murder and Piper's assault. Heart racing, she zoomed in on a photograph of Elena.

Curly blonde hair, blue eyes. Petite and slender.

Their face shape was similar as was the curve of their lips. The resemblance was uncanny. They could be sisters. Additionally, they'd grown up in the same neighborhood. And Elena was nineteen, one year older than Piper had been at the time of her assault.

An icy finger of dread touched the back of Piper's neck.

No. It couldn't be.

With trembling fingers, she called Derek on video chat. Her boss picked up on the first ring. He was in his office, a stack of paperwork in front of him. The top button of his uniform was undone and his sleeves were rolled up. He offered her a smile with his greeting, but it was strained with exhaustion at the edges. "What's up?"

"Lionel Islip was the man who attacked me, right? You're certain?"

Derek froze for a moment, the question obviously catching him off guard. "Yes. Why?"

"I'll explain, but take me through it. Why are you so convinced?"

"His fingerprints were all over the house. He'd made threats against you several times, had a violent history with women, and was known for breaking into houses to steal things. Neighbors reported seeing him in the area at the time of the assault. We found your necklace in his bedroom." Derek's tone was gentle and reassuring. "It was him, Piper. I'm certain."

She desperately wanted to believe him. Derek wasn't just her boss, he was also her friend. He'd known her since she was a teen, and when her mother brought home another loser or began using drugs again, he'd rescued Piper from more dangerous situations than she could count. He was the epitome of a caring, thorough, and dedicated law enforcement officer.

But they'd never talked about her case. Not really. Piper had never needed to, but now those niggles of doubt in the back of her mind wouldn't be silenced. "You didn't get a confession."

Lionel had pulled a gun on the police when they drove up to his house to arrest him. Derek had nearly been shot during the incident. She hadn't known that at the time. She'd been trapped inside her own fear, running as far away from Rock Fort as her rusted-out Ford would take her. It was only later, after moving back home, that she learned how close Derek had come to losing his life to get justice in her case.

Piper forced herself to say the words lingering on her tongue. "Is it possible you got it wrong, Derek? Lionel's fingerprints were in our house, but he had been my mother's boyfriend for months before they finally broke up. He could've stolen my necklace at any time, and I never saw the attacker's face since he wore a mask."

Derek was quiet for a long moment. "Is there something you aren't telling me?"

"Jackson is convinced Elena's killer is coming after me because he's afraid I witnessed something in the woods, but what if that's not true?" She fumbled around in her laptop bag before removing a copy of Elena's driver's license photo. Piper held it up next to her. "Look at us. We could be sisters. Elena lived in my old neighborhood, was roughly the same age as I was at the time of my assault, and the perpetrator beat her before shooting her."

The image of a masked man standing over her in the kitchen, the gun in his hand, flashed in her mind. Her heart rate increased.

Piper shoved the memory away and continued, "Yes, there are differences. He lured her to a field before assaulting her, but the perpetrator could've adapted his methods. There are enough similarities between my attack and Elena's murder that I have a sick pit in my stomach. So, I'm asking because I need to be sure."

Derek met her gaze. There wasn't a trace of anger, only sympathy. The sheriff's badge on his shirt shimmered in the fluorescent lighting and this tone was authoritative and confident. "I'm sure, Piper. The man who killed Elena is not the same one who attacked you."

She let go of the breath she was holding. Her mind was conjuring theories and horrors that weren't based in reality. It'd been ten years since her assault. The attacker wouldn't have waited so long before striking again. Someone like this kept going until they were dead or in prison. So yes, there were similarities between her case and Elena's, but two very different perpetrators.

Piper rubbed her forehead. "I'm sorry, Derek. I... well, there's no reasonable explanation for my paranoia. Chalk it up to being shot at today." She dropped her hand and gave him a weak smile. "It won't happen again."

"Never apologize for testing plausible theories. I know Jackson is worried about the attack today, and I understand his logic, but I've questioned Marcus and there's nothing to indicate he purposefully targeted you. He was high and not in his right mind. I don't think there was any rhyme or reason to what he did."

His observation confirmed Piper's initial theory. Some of the tension left her shoulders.

"Deputies questioned the gun shops in town," Derek continued. "No one sold Marcus the Glock, which means someone must've given it to him. I'm working on figuring out who." He tilted his head. "Get some sleep, Piper. You look worn out."

"Pot meet kettle."

"Yeah, but I'm the boss. Someone has to keep this department running." Derek's mouth quirked up. "I have an explanation for your paranoia. Finn must be driving you crazy with that piano music. He's played the same notes fifteen times since we started this conversation."

"Has he? I learned to tune him out."

"Good for you. I'd go batty listening to that for hours on end." Derek's words were critical, but his tone was full of affection. "He's determined. I'll give him that." He paused. "How's Ava?"

Piper arched a slight brow. "She's doing well. The doctor says she may be cleared to drive next week." She glanced up to make sure her sister wasn't within earshot. "You know, if you have a crush on Ava, you could ask her out. It'll be easier than keeping track of her through me."

Derek's cheeks heated. "I don't have a crush on Ava. I'm just being neighborly."

"Of course you are. Just like you were being neighborly when you fixed the gutters last week. Or when you brought her flowers when she was in the hospital. And all those home-cooked meals—"

"Cut it out." He rolled his eyes. "I'm a nice guy. That's all."

"My sister could use a nice guy." Piper couldn't believe she was playing matchmaker, but Ava and the kids had been through a lot. They deserved someone solid and dependable. Someone who'd take care of them. Piper had seen Ava and Derek flirt from time to time. She knew her sister was interested, so she didn't feel the least bit guilty in meddling.

Heaven knew, Ava would do it in a heartbeat.

"I... We're friends and I don't want to screw that up..." Derek seemed to struggle for a moment, and then he shuffled some paperwork on his desk. His cheeks were fire-engine red. "We shouldn't be talking about this. Forget I brought it up. See you in the morning."

After he hung up, Piper said a silent prayer that Derek would find the courage to ask Ava out. The two would make a great couple. Then her gaze landed on Elena's photograph. She breathed out, the twist in her stomach making it ache. She added to her prayer, "God, I really want to find Elena's killer. Help guide me."

Moxie came running around the corner and nudged Piper's hand with his nose before walking to the door and standing next to it. Finn was still banging away on the piano. Now, the notes were getting on her nerves.

She rose from her chair. "Looking for peace and quiet, boy?"

He barked in reply. Piper shrugged on her coat before

opening the back door. Moxie took off into the yard as she stepped onto the porch. Derek's assurances had gone a long way to making her feel better. Still, there was no harm in doing a perimeter check of the property.

Cool air caressed her cheeks. A full moon was out, painting the neighborhood in an ethereal glow. Piper kept an eye on Moxie as she circled the house to the front yard. The Labrador pranced beside her. "Don't get into anything you aren't supposed to. I'm not giving you a bath because you bothered a skunk."

She could swear he grinned in reply before stopping to sniff at some bushes bordering their property line. Piper reached the driveway. The street was quiet. Overhead an owl hooted. She breathed in the crisp air and let the silence wash over her. Exhaustion seeped into her muscles. Derek was right, she was tired and should go to bed.

An unfamiliar vehicle at the end of the street caught her attention. It hid in the shadows. An SUV judging from the size. The front-end was angled toward her house, giving anyone in the driver's seat a perfect view of her property.

Piper's pulse skittered and her fingers brushed against the weapon at her hip as she eased down the driveway. The feeling she was being watched this morning might not have been in her head after all. She lengthened her strides, intent on confronting whoever was in the SUV.

Moxie shot ahead of her. Before she could call the mutt back, the driver's side door opened.

A man emerged.

Her hand tightened on her weapon as she undid the button on her holster. "Rock Fort Sheriff's Department. Identify yourself."

Moxie barked with excitement.

"It's me, Piper." Jackson stepped into the moonlight. He'd shed his cowboy hat and his jacket. A button-down shirt molded to his broad shoulders and accented his narrow waist. Tousled hair and a five-o'clock shadow added a rough edge to his appearance that was all too appealing.

Attraction shot through Piper, fueling her irritation. "What are you doing here?"

He patted Moxie, who was dancing around seeking attention. "Keeping an eye on things."

"That's unnecessary. Derek interviewed Marcus and confirmed he wasn't targeting me. The attack was random."

"He told me."

"Then?"

He shrugged, as if to say it didn't matter, and his mouth quirked. "Don't worry, Piper. I've done stakeouts under rougher conditions. The seat in my SUV leans back, I've brought snacks, and there are a ton of reports to go through. Chances are, it'll be a quiet and boring night." Jackson leaned against his vehicle. "What did you find out from Elena's social media accounts?"

He was attempting to distract her with the case. Piper didn't intend to veer off track for very long. "There's a woman who pops up frequently. Kylie Reynolds. She and

Elena lived in the same neighborhood, a few streets away from each other. I think we should interview Kylie in the morning. We can also question some neighbors. If Shawn and Elena were having an affair, maybe someone saw him going and coming from her house."

"Good idea. In the meantime, my boss, Lieutenant Rodriguez, has assigned some additional rangers to aid in the investigation. They'll be here tomorrow afternoon." Jackson turned away. "See you in the morning."

"Wait..." She leveled him with a stern look and crossed her arms over her chest. "This is ridiculous. In case you haven't noticed, I'm a trained law enforcement officer. There's no reason for you to stand guard outside my house. I can handle things myself."

"I never said you couldn't."

"Then why—"

"Why do you think?" Jackson snapped. "I care, okay, Piper? There, I said it out loud. I care about you. In spite of everything, and as foolish as it makes me, I still care. You were nearly shot to death in front of me today. Do you really think I can get a good night's sleep at the hotel? It would be impossible. I'd lay in bed and worry that some lunatic was heading to your house to kill you."

Her heart squeezed tight. Without thinking, Piper stepped forward until she had her arms wrapped around his waist. His breath hitched and then Jackson returned her embrace. His arms were warm, his presence steady. Nothing was going to hurt her tonight. Not under his watch.

Relief swamped her, causing unexpected and

unbidden tears. She was scared. Terrified, actually. It didn't make sense. There was no evidence anyone was targeting her, and yet, the last two days had left her on edge.

Jackson pulled her closer. His heart thumped against her ear. She didn't deserve this. Didn't deserve him. She was damaged goods with a cloud of trouble that followed in her wake. It'd been true ten years ago. It was still true today.

Piper wrestled with the emotions threatening to overwhelm her. She should put a stop to this, but there was no wall big enough to keep Jackson out of her heart.

She swallowed hard. "I care about you too."

"I know. If you didn't, you wouldn't fight so hard to keep me at a distance. Jensen."

She huffed out a laugh. "I knew something was bothering you this afternoon."

His lips brushed against the top of her head. "Go inside, Piper. We have a lot of work to do tomorrow. One of us has to be conscious enough to interview Kylie Reynolds."

She reluctantly stepped out of his embrace. "I feel bad leaving you out here."

"Don't. It's my decision." He gently turned her toward the house. "And take Moxie with you. I'm covered in dog slobber."

"Ewww. You hugged me."

"Actually, you hugged me." He winked. "See you in the morning."

Piper whistled for the dog before crossing the street

back toward her house. She reached the front door, and with one last glance at Jackson's vehicle, ducked inside. The locks slid home easily. Piper armed the alarm. Then she parted the curtain to view the street.

Quiet. No sign of trouble. She was safe. Locked inside her house, with an alarm on, and a Texas Ranger standing guard. Still a sense of overwhelming dread pressed on her sternum. It'd plagued her since the move back to Rock Fort and, after Elena's murder, had only gotten worse. It wasn't logical. The conversation with Derek should have silenced all her doubts. Her attacker was six feet underground in the cemetery. She was safe.

So why on earth did she feel so scared?

ELEVEN

Kylie Reynolds lived in a double-wide trailer perched on cement blocks. Folding chairs were scattered in the brown grass around a homemade firepit. A hammock, chewed by the squirrels, hung broken from an oak tree, and the wooden front porch looked ready to collapse.

Jackson swigged his takeaway coffee, hoping to wake up his exhausted brain cells. There hadn't been a lick of trouble at Piper's, and he'd left at dawn to catch a few hours of sleep. He was tired, but adrenaline would keep him going. This wasn't the first case he'd worked day and night to solve.

He eyed the older model Chevy truck in the dirt driveway. "That's Kylie's vehicle. Looks like she's home."

Piper hummed in reply, but her gaze was locked on something farther down the street. Her complexion was unusually pale. Jackson leaned over to see what had caught her attention. His heart skittered. This was Piper's old neighborhood. In fact, they were on her street. If he hadn't been so tired, he might've realized it earlier.

Her mom's trailer hunched at the end of the road. Time had not been good to it. Rust climbed the siding like a swarm of bugs. Cement blocks and random car parts peeked out from the overgrown weeds taking over the property. A dented mailbox perched at the end of the drive.

Piper's expression was blank, her posture loose, but underlying the calm exterior was a well-hidden tension. She hadn't lived there at the time of the attack, but was staying with Grandma Mary. Still, she'd often go to her mother's trailer to visit or clean or deliver groceries. It was while doing one of those small acts of kindness, she'd been attacked. Lionel Islip, one of her mother's exes, had entered through the broken back door, beaten her, and then pointed his gun at her. It was only the unexpected arrival of her mother that saved Piper's life.

Sadly, that hadn't been the first violent or abusive thing that'd happened to Piper in that house. It was just the worst.

Jackson placed a comforting hand on her arm.

Piper flinched.

He quickly removed it. "Sorry."

Embarrassment heated her cheeks. She blinked and then straightened her shoulders. "Come on. We have to interview Kylie."

Before he could respond, she flung open the door and got out of the car. Jackson was tempted to call her back, but what would be the point? She'd never admit that her

PTSD was triggered by being in this neighborhood, so close to her mother's house. It left him feeling helpless and frustrated. He didn't know how to help her, and in the past, any hint of comfort he offered only made things worse.

Piper iced him out. She always had whenever things got hard. Except... last night had been different. She'd hugged him like he was her anchor in the storm. Jackson wasn't sure what had cracked through her outer defenses, but he wanted to figure it out.

A dangerous proposition. He was likely to end up brokenhearted for his trouble.

Shaking off the train of thoughts, he joined Piper on the sidewalk, and together, they approached Kylie's trailer. Jackson punched the doorbell, but when nothing chimed inside the house, he gave a swift knock on the worn wooden door. The sound of a baby crying drew closer, along with shuffled footsteps. The curtain at the window shifted. Moments later, the door swung open revealing a dark-haired woman with a child on her hip. Kylie. Jackson recognized her instantly from her driver's license photo.

Her chin trembled and a tear leaked from one eye. "You're here about Elena."

"Yes, ma'am." He introduced himself and Piper. "We were hoping to ask you a few questions. May we come in?"

Kylie stepped back. Nineteen, with a rail thin figure and acne scars, she was dressed in sweatpants two sizes too big and a cropped T-shirt. A green-and-yellow bruise marred the curve of her chin. A fresher mark, deep purple and painful looking, marched down her left arm. Judging from the shape and size, a man had grabbed her. Hard.

Jackson glanced at Piper. He could tell by the way her lips flattened that she'd seen the marks on Kylie too. The young woman's eyes were also puffy and red, as if she'd been sobbing as hard as the baby when they knocked on the door. The little one wailed, the bow in her thin hair bouncing with the force of her cries.

He crossed over the threshold, careful to look behind the door at his blind spot. No sound emanated from the rear of the house. The space was tiny, a living room and kitchen area connected by a small dining table. It smelled of burned coffee, even though a window in the kitchen was wide open. Dirty dishes piled on the counter.

"Is anyone home with you, ma'am?" Jackson asked.

"No. My mom is at work." She hitched the baby higher on her hip and reached for a pacifier on an end table.

Piper shut the door. She smiled sympathetically at Kylie, even as her gaze discreetly scanned the surroundings, just like Jackson. "How old is she? Six months?"

"Seven." Kylie worked the pacifier into the baby's mouth as she sat on a threadbare couch covered in piles of clothes. The child quieted, laying her head down on Kylie's shoulder. "Jennifer is teething and it's made for a lot of sleepless nights." She sighed heavily and more tears leaked from her eyes. She wiped them away. "I heard about what happened to Elena yesterday from a neighbor. I still can't believe it. Was she really murdered?"

Piper gently pushed aside a pile of clothing and sat on the edge of the couch. "I'm afraid so. How well did you know Elena?"

"Since we were kids. We grew up together. She is…" Kylie bit her lip. "Was my best friend."

Jackson positioned himself against the wall, with a view of the hallway leading to the bedrooms, the kitchen, and the front door. No noise emanated from the rear of the house. Kylie was likely telling the truth about being home alone. But he wouldn't let down his guard. Someone had put those marks on the young woman and any man willing to do that… well, he was volatile and dangerous.

"Elena was the sweetest person." Kylie swiped at another tear as it trailed down her cheek. "Why would anyone want to hurt her?"

"We were hoping you could tell us."

She blew out a breath. "Elena never did anything she wasn't supposed to. I was the rebel. Parties and skipping school and all that nonsense. Got myself pregnant at eighteen." She adjusted her hold on the baby. Grief thickened her voice and new tears welled. "I used to make fun of Elena for being such a stick-in-the-mud, but she's the one who really came to my rescue when I got pregnant. She helped me get a job at the grocery store. When all my party friends bailed on me and Jennifer's father didn't want to help, it was Elena who stuck by my side."

Jackson had learned a long time ago to keep his own

emotions in check when interviewing a witness or a victim. But there were times when it was hard. "It sounds like she was a very good friend to you."

"She was."

"Do you know if Elena was dating anyone?"

Kylie swiped at her cheeks and worried her bottom lip. "She had a boyfriend for a while, but they broke up. She never told me his name. I got the sense it was new, and she didn't want to introduce him to her friends before she'd decided if he was a keeper. Elena was pretty picky about the guys she would date. She was also private. I assumed he was someone who attended college with her."

Or it was someone she *had* to keep secret. Like Shawn, who was a married man. If Elena grew tired of being the other woman, and threatened to expose the affair, Shawn would be embarrassed, and his wife humiliated. Townsfolk would talk.

Jackson kept his posture relaxed and his tone even. "Do you know when they broke up?"

"No. I was dealing with my own drama and didn't pry into hers. I knew she'd tell me when she was ready."

Piper gestured to the marks on Kylie's arm. Her tone was gentle. "Is that the drama you're talking about?"

Kylie glanced at the bruises and her gaze skittered across the living room. "I left him. For good this time. Living with my mom isn't easy, but Jennifer and I are better off here."

"You can press charges."

She jerked her head and clung to her baby. "It's

Jennifer's father. I won't do that unless it becomes necessary. So far, he's left us alone. That's good enough for me." Her eyes widened. "Oh…" Kylie's hand flew up to cover her mouth.

"What?"

She shook her head. "It's nothing…"

"Why don't you tell me anyway," Piper kept her tone reassuring and her demeanor nonjudgmental, but there was a tilt to her posture indicating she knew whatever Kylie was about to say was important. "I can decide if it matters or not."

Kylie was quiet for a long moment. She hugged her daughter closer. "Elena helped me leave my ex. She snuck over while he was at work and watched the baby while I loaded my stuff into her car." She swallowed hard. "But I don't think he would do anything to hurt her. I mean… I'm the one he'd be mad at, right?"

Jackson wasn't convinced of that. He'd seen abusers attack people who assisted the victim escape. Isolation was important in order to maintain control. A friend or family member willing to step up… that was a threat that needed to be eliminated.

Men had killed for less. A lot less.

TWELVE

Piper hesitated on Kylie's front step. Warm sunshine beat down on her shoulders as she pulled a business card from her pocket. "Leaving your ex was a brave thing to do." She extended the card. "If he gives you any trouble, call me."

Kylie hitched the baby up higher on her hip and took the card. The bruises on her arm were deep purple and looked painful. Jennifer tugged on a lock of her mom's hair with one chubby finger. The baby was lucky to have a mother who put her first. Piper hadn't been so fortunate. She'd do whatever was necessary to support the young woman in getting her life together.

She flipped through the stack of business cards she kept along with her own. "There are programs for housing and support groups for survivors of domestic violence. My friend, Mariana Garcia, is a social worker. She can help." Piper found Mariana's card and extended it to Kylie. "Here's her number. Can I pass on your information to her? Mariana will put together a packet and even help you fill out the forms."

This time, Kylie hesitated. "I don't want a handout."

"It's a hand up. You've done the hard part by leaving a bad situation. There's no shame in getting the support you need to make a better life for you and Jennifer."

"It's charity."

Piper smothered her irritation. She couldn't fault Kylie for her pride. After all, she shared it. Accepting help had never been her strong suit. But stubbornness could get the young woman—and possibly her daughter—killed. Abusers were chameleons. One moment, they were charming and loving, the next violent and terrifying. "My mom dated men like your ex. People tried to help her repeatedly. She refused, and eventually, I paid the price for it alongside her."

She let that sink in and then continued, "You're so much stronger than you know, and maybe you'll get there without a helping hand, but I promise it'll be easier if you have people in your corner rooting for you." She extended the card farther toward Kylie. "Do it. For Jennifer, if not for yourself."

Kylie hesitated once more and then nodded. She took the card, fingering it. "Are there programs for getting your GED?"

"I'm sure there are. Mariana would be happy to help with that. I'll have her call you in the next day or two."

"Okay. Thanks."

Piper gave a wave to the baby and a smile to Kylie before turning to join Jackson in the driveway. In his cowboy hat and sunglasses, he cut an impressive figure. She kept her gaze on him to avoid looking at her mom's house. Being back on her old street, seeing the trailer she'd grown up in, had triggered memories of the assault. Piper's PTSD was flaring back to life. Once again, she was reminded that Elena's murder had unearthed her own tragic past in an unsettling way.

Jackson hung up his cell phone, a frustrated expression on his face. "Well, Kylie's ex, Wally Hutchinson, hasn't been to work for the last three days. Deputies went to his house, but it's closed up tight. A Dodge RAM is registered to him. No sign of it. I've put a BOLO out on the vehicle."

"Let's go talk to his younger brother. Todd lives on the same street as Elena."

The drive took less than a minute. Piper's nerves settled the moment they turned off her childhood street. Elena's house sat at the end of the block. It was a cute, modular home with white shutters and a red front door. Carefully tended flower beds with bright wind spinners dotted the yard.

In contrast, Todd Hutchinson's house, three doors down, desperately needed an overhaul. Beer cans littered the yard, alongside broken-down car parts. An ancient sedan sat on bricks. Weeds grew wild and untamed. A pit bull attached with a long chain to a dog house, languished behind a broken chain-link fence encircling the backyard. Piper carefully skirted a pile of unknown objects on her way to the front door.

Jackson kept pace alongside her. His hand rested on his holster, his gaze shifting back and forth. "I hate this."

She knew exactly what he meant. Sunshine beamed down on them, but there was a creepy vibe to the house that instinctually made her want to run in the other direction. Like there were eyes on them. She'd checked for cameras but didn't see any. It was possible they were hidden, but Todd didn't seem like the kind to spend his money on security.

The front porch was a slab of broken concrete. The screen door hung by one hinge, the interior wooden door open. Somewhere inside, a television blared. Piper rapped on the doorframe. "Mr. Hutchinson? Todd Hutchinson?"

Footsteps approached. Todd materialized out of the darkness like a bat emerging from his cave. He blinked at the sudden sunlight. His clothes were rumpled and his hair mussed. In one hand, he held a can of beer. "Whatdaya want, Piper?"

"We'd like to speak to you about Elena Harris."

The screen door creaked open, and Todd exited the house. It was hard to believe she'd gone to high school with this man. Granted, he'd been a few years ahead of her, but still... the last years hadn't been good to him. He'd gained weight, all in his belly, and his hair was thinning. A prominent forehead swept down into a long nose and thin lips. His features had always reminded her of a rat. Or maybe it was his personality. Todd was as sneaky and as slippery as they came.

Beside her, she felt rather than heard Jackson inhale.

Obviously, he hadn't recognized Todd's name, but he must've remembered his face. It was distinctive.

Todd took a long swig of his beer. "I heard she was murdered. Don't know nothing about that."

"Really? I'm surprised. Your brother had beef with her."

His gaze narrowed. "Wally? What's he got to do with this?"

Piper shrugged. "Rumors are spreading, Todd. I'm hearing things. I don't want to believe a word of it, mind you, but it seems your brother has up and run off. Wally hasn't been to work in days and he's not at home. I was hoping you could tell me where he is."

He sniffed and rubbed a dirty hand under his nose. "I ain't my brother's keeper, Piper."

"Understood. Have you heard from him recently?"

"We hung out a few days ago. Wally was upset cuz his girlfriend up and left with the baby. I took him out for drinks to forget about her at the Watering Hole."

"What day was this?"

Todd scratched the back of his neck. "Must've been Wednesday. Wally met someone while we were there. Some tall beauty with a nice body. He took off on me. I ain't seen him since." He tossed back the rest of his beer, crushed the can with a meaty hand, and tossed it into the yard. "He'll pop back up eventually."

Wednesday was the same day Elena was murdered. Piper made a mental note to check with the Watering Hole and confirm the Hutchinson brothers were there. "What time did you and Wally go to the bar?"

"Around noon. He took off work early."

"And what time did you leave?"

He shrugged. "Don't know. Maybe six or seven."

"What about Wally?"

"No idea. Like I said, he hooked up with some pretty young thing."

"Happen to catch her name?"

"No. I was busy getting some action from a redhead who was crying over her own breakup."

"Right, well, if you do hear from Wally, tell him to call me." Piper locked eyes with Todd. "It's important. I don't want him to get into any trouble because he ignored me."

He flashed a savage smile. "Sure thing, Piper. And hey, anytime you want to slum it with someone in your old neighborhood, give me a call." He tugged at his pants in a lewd manner. "I'll show you a good time."

Jackson was standing close enough, Piper felt his muscles tense. His eyes weren't visible behind the lenses of his dark sunglasses, but she imagined he was staring Todd down. To his credit though, his expression remained impassive. He stood back and let her handle it.

Piper simply rolled her eyes. It wasn't the first time one of the Hutchinsons had made a pass at her. She'd grown up in this neighborhood and had dodged several of their advances. "Bye, Todd."

"See ya around, Piper."

Todd never glanced at Jackson. The screen door creaked, and he disappeared back into the dark house. Piper tilted her head to indicate they should walk back toward Elena's house. Once they were out of earshot, she said, "Breathe, Jackson. You look mad enough to spit nails."

He exhaled forcefully. "You handled it well, but the way he was looking at you... I'm not ashamed to admit, I wanted to toss him right over the porch railing and teach him some manners." Jackson slanted a glance at her. "We went to high school with him."

"Yep. He was a junior when we were freshman but dropped out mid-year and never came back. His brother, Wally, is about eight years older than Todd. Both of them have been arrested for drug possession, fighting, petty theft, and domestic violence. Neither man is anyone I'd meet in a nature preserve parking lot like Elena did. Especially Wally. She knew he'd beaten her friend."

"We don't know how the killer lured her to the parking lot."

"True."

Piper reached Elena's front door. Using the key taken from the evidence locker, she undid the lock. Deputies had found her car and house keys in the field on the night she died. Piper then slid on a pair of gloves. Pinpricks of nerves traveled up her spine. She glanced over her shoulder at Todd's house. There was no sign of the man, but she felt eyes on her all the same.

"Yeah. I feel it too." Jackson rolled his shoulders and pulled on his own set of gloves. "Todd?"

"Maybe." Piper wasn't happy they were being watched, but it was a relief to know Jackson had the same feeling. Otherwise, she might question her own instincts.

She pushed open the door and crossed the threshold. The blinds were open, sunlight playing along the shag carpet and the 90s-style couch. An open floor plan enabled Piper to view most of the kitchen and the tiny dining room. The compressor on the ancient fridge fired up. It sounded like an airplane.

"Do you think Wally was hiding in his brother's house?" Jackson entered behind her and shut the door. "I didn't hear or see anyone else, but it was so dark inside the house, he could've been listening and we didn't realize it."

Piper half-heard him. Her attention was drawn to something under the coffee table. She stepped farther into the living room, tilting her head to get a better look at the black mass. "Jackson, what is that?"

He pushed past her and crouched down. His brow creased in concentration. And then, in the span of a heartbeat, fear widened his eyes. "Run, Piper!"

She didn't bother to ask for an explanation. She bolted for the door and flung it open.

A blast of heat hit and a violent force blew her off her feet.

THIRTEEN

The explosion tossed Piper in the air like a rag doll.

Intense heat swept over her like a tidal wave. Pain exploded along her shoulder and hip as she crashed to the unyielding ground and rolled. Her body collided with Jackson's vehicle and came to a bone-jarring stop. Her chest was tight, her heart pounding. She couldn't breathe. For several seconds, she lay there stunned, staring at the tire in front of her face. Her handgun, strapped to her waist, dug into her side. Debris fell around her. She barely registered it.

Spots danced across her vision. The explosion had knocked the wind from her lungs and it was a struggle to take in air. Piper drew in a shallow breath. Then another. Finally, her brain kicked into gear and was able to control her body. Ears ringing, she pushed off the cement driveway into a sitting position.

Elena's house was engulfed in flames. Parts of the

roof and the building were scattered everywhere. In the yard. Down the street. Fear reached up and stole the air Piper had worked so hard to pull into her lungs.

Jackson. Where was Jackson?

She screamed his name. Or thought she did. It was hard to hear anything over the ringing in her ears. Piper moved to stand and pain vibrated through her arm. She glanced at her shoulder and realized she was bleeding. Her shirt was ripped, a chunk of flesh missing from her arm. Dizziness hit her. She had no issue with injuries on other people, but the sight of her own blood... it was traumatic. A reminder of the assault.

Shoving aside the pain, Piper used the car for support as she maneuvered into a standing position. White hot agony shot through her left knee. She shifted, immediately taking the pressure off, while scanning for Jackson. Smoke billowed from the house and was carried on the wind, making it impossible to see farther than several inches in front of her face.

Please, God. Please let him be all right.

"Jackson!" The cry was followed by a fit of coughing as the thick smoke entered her lungs. She bent over to drag in a breath and yelled again. Tears filmed her eyes. Another side effect of the smoke. "Jackson."

He'd been right behind her. Seconds. Only seconds. But in this particular instance, seconds mattered.

Suddenly, the wind shifted. The smoke cleared as it blew away from Piper toward the woods along the back of Elena's property. A large form appeared. It grew closer, and as Piper wiped the tears from her eyes, Jackson came into view. His face was blackened by soot, his shirt torn along the chest, and blood dripped from a cut on his cheek. But he was alive.

Relief rippled through her with such intensity she had to use the SUV to hold herself up. More tears filmed her eyes, and this time, Piper couldn't blame them on the smoke. Crying had never been her thing. She'd done it maybe five times in her entire adult life, but the thought of Jackson not being okay... it hit her hard.

He got close enough, and she threw her arms around him. Jackson held her for a long moment, his strong and tender embrace unleashing every buried emotion inside her. She pulled back to look him in the face and had the insane urge to plant a kiss on his lips. The heat from the blaze and the smoke stinging her eyes held her back.

His mouth moved, but she couldn't make out the words over the ringing in her ears. Piper swallowed. Her mouth tasted like sand. "I can't hear you."

It sounded like she was shouting in her head, but she doubted Jackson could hear her any more than she could hear him. His gaze swept over the injury on her shoulder and then he wrapped an arm around her waist and pointed to the end of the driveway. Yes, they needed to get a safer distance away from the fire. Sweat beaded across her skin. The heat from the flames was intense.

Piper took a step and nearly hit the ground as her hurt knee gave out. The next moment, she was lifted off the ground by Jackson. Muscles along his chest rippled as he pulled her closer. Instantly she was sheltered. Cared for. He carried her across the street as if she weighed nothing, and that sent an uncharacteristic wave of femininity through her.

Jackson had always had that effect on her. He had this way of taking care of her without taking advantage. Protecting without being domineering. He was a man confident in his skin. Had always been, even at eighteen. Piper rarely let down her guard, but Jackson was her weakness. Obviously, he still was.

An elderly woman materialized in front of them. She wore a housedress and slippers, her gray hair clipped short to frame a mahogany face. Winnie Wainwright. Worry clouded her dark eyes and created lines between her brows. She waved Jackson forward and held open the screen door to her home. Seconds later, Piper was deposited on a kitchen chair.

Jackson bent down next to her. "How badly are you hurt?"

Finally, she could hear him. The ringing was still there but fading. "It's not bad. My knee got banged up and this scrape on my arm probably needs stitches, but I'll live." She lightly touched the cut on his cheek. "You?"

"I'm fine." Jackson's gaze shot to the windows overlooking the street before returning to focus on her. "Elena's house was searched by investigators on the night she died. Whoever planted that bomb did it after they left."

A shudder rippled down her spine. "The bomber was nearby. Watching us."

"Yes. The device was controlled by a remote detonator. This was a targeted attack."

Horror sank into Piper. This case had gone from murder to bombing. Things were escalating quickly.

Winnie returned with a first aid kit. "I've called the police. They're on the way, along with EMS." She clicked her tongue as her gaze took in the gash on Piper's arm. "That needs to be cleaned immediately."

Winnie had been a school nurse before her retirement. Her husband's cancer diagnosis had wiped out their savings, leaving her with little after he passed. She'd moved into the trailer park shortly after Piper turned ten. Many nights, when things at home were too much, she'd camped out on Winnie's couch. She still came by regularly to visit her.

"I'm going to leave you in Mrs. Wainwright's capable hands." Jackson rose. "I need to check on the other neighbors. Make sure no one else was injured."

Piper pushed against the chair. "I'll help—"

Jackson stopped her with a hand on her shoulder. "You're hurt and I'll work faster if I know you're getting the treatment you need." His gaze bounced to Winnie before latching onto to hers. "Please."

His unspoken message was received loud and clear. Piper was likely the target of the attack. Jackson still believed Marcus had been sent to shoot her yesterday morning. In light of the bombing, she had to admit, he could be right. Piper settled back into the chair. "Be careful."

"Always."

He flashed her a smile that warmed her insides before turning to leave. The screen door slammed shut behind him.

Winnie approached with a bottle of antiseptic and cotton pads. She winced slightly. "This may hurt."

"It's all right." Piper settled against the wooden chair, bracing herself for the pain. Every muscle in her body ached, and she knew the soreness would last for days. Soot covered Winnie's floor. "Thank you for fixing me up. I'm sorry about the mess."

"Nonsense, child. I'm just glad you and Jackson are okay."

She poured the liquid over the gash on Piper's arm. White hot agony shot through her. She inhaled sharply. The best thing for the pain was a distraction. "Did you know Elena?"

"Of course. Good girl. Her mama's pride and joy." She poured more antiseptic. "Bessie was a good friend of mine, God rest her soul, and after she passed, I did my best to look after Elena." Winnie's mouth turned down as a film of tears appeared in her eyes. "I know how cruel life is, and death shouldn't shock me anymore, but it hurts that someone would murder such a sweet young woman."

Piper reached out and patted the older woman's hand. "It should hurt. When it stops hurting is when we've lost something of ourselves."

Winnie nodded. "I suppose that's true."

Piper winced as Winnie gently cleaned the wound.

"What did Elena think of her job at the Kingston Law Firm?"

"She liked it. The pay was good and the schedule allowed her to take classes at the community college at night. The Kingstons are a hard bunch, but I have to admit they treat their staff well."

She weighed her options. Winnie wasn't a gossip, and so far, questioning Elena's friends hadn't gotten them very far. Maybe it was time to be more direct. "I heard a rumor that Elena was secretly involved with Shawn Kingston."

Winnie froze and then her mouth pursed. "Well, that explains a lot."

"What do you mean?"

"I knew Elena had a boyfriend, but she wouldn't say who. It worried me. Elena was a hard worker, but even though she'd grown up in this neighborhood, she was a touch naïve. Bessie sheltered her from a lot." She huffed out a breath. "Shawn Kingston takes after his daddy. That man couldn't stay faithful to his wife if you gave him a million dollars. Guess the apple doesn't fall too far from the tree in this case."

"Did Elena ever complain about the relationship with her boyfriend?"

"No. I got the sense it wasn't serious."

That made sense since Shawn was married. It was well known most of the Kingston men were womanizers. Maybe Elena understood it was a fling and had no intention of exposing Shawn. Having an affair was morally questionable, but it wasn't a crime.

Piper gritted her teeth against a fresh wave of pain as Winnie continued cleaning her wound. "I also heard Elena helped a friend escape her abusive boyfriend."

"She did. Wally Hutchinson is as mean as a rattlesnake and just as toxic. His brother, Todd, ain't much better. A'course, I understand their childhood was awful. Their daddy was scary. But there comes a point when a man has to decide for himself who he's going to be." She ripped open a package of gauze. "Wally wasn't too happy with Elena for meddling in his affairs. He confronted her on the street last week as she was leaving for work, yelling and screaming about how she needs to mind her own business."

"Did she report the incident to the police?"

"Not to my knowledge. With a man like Wally, sometimes going to the police escalates things rather than helps matters."

Piper curled her hands into fists as frustration bubbled. She understood Elena's logic, but she wished the woman would've reported him. "Was that all Wally did?"

Winnie stuck a bandage on her wound and sealed the edges down. "I'm not sure. The day before she died, Elena came to my house and dropped off her tablet and some other items for safekeeping. She was nervous. She felt like someone was watching her and suspected her house had been broken into. I urged her to report the matter to the police, and she swore she would, but—"

Her voice broke off. Piper understood why.

Elena hadn't reported the incidents to the police because she'd been murdered before she could.

Her mind whirled. If Elena was being stalked, her home broken into... then why on earth did she meet her killer in the nature preserve? It made little sense. Unless the person she thought she was meeting was a friend. Or her ex-boyfriend, Shawn.

But then why bomb her house? Unless... unless the person was afraid of what Piper and Jackson would find.

Elena's killer had taken her cell phone. That simple act had stalled their investigation. What if the killer had previously broken into her house to steal her tablet? Text messages, phone calls, internet searches... most people stored them on a cloud service so they could be easily accessed across devices.

Piper's heart sped up. "Mrs. Wainwright, I need to take Elena's tablet, along with the other personal items she left you."

"Of course, dear. Let me get them."

She shuffled off to the back room and then quickly returned with a jewelry box, a stack of bills, and a tablet. The wail of sirens showed backup had arrived, along with the fire department.

Piper lifted the device. It was charged. The screen glowed, the background a lovely Texas sunset, but in order to unlock it, she needed Elena's fingerprint or a passcode.

She winced. Most devices with biometric fingerprint locks required electrical conduction, meaning the reader sensed the faint electrical charge running through a person's skin. Elena's tablet was one of them. Once she died, it was impossible to open the tablet with her fingerprint.

Piper blew out a breath and glanced at Winnie. It was a long shot, but she had to ask. "I don't suppose you know the passcode."

The old woman's face broke into a soft smile. "Actually, I do."

FOURTEEN

Hours later, Jackson sipped water while waiting for the task force meeting to start. He'd taken a shower to wash off the smoke smell and changed his clothes, but his body ached from being thrown during the explosion at Elena's house. Thankfully, no one was seriously injured by the blast. Including Piper.

She sat in the chair next to him at the conference room table. Her hair was pulled back into a tight ponytail that accented her high cheekbones and the long column of her throat. A faint scratch marred her ear and her complexion was pale. Like him, she'd showered and changed her clothes. Jackson's insides clenched as he imagined how close they'd come to dying. A few seconds more and neither of them would be sitting at this table now.

Thank you, God, for protecting us.

It was the second time in two days Piper had been in

mortal danger. First the shooting and then the bombing. Jackson didn't believe either was a coincidence. He couldn't prove it yet, but he trusted his own instincts. Whoever was behind this would try again. And again. Until the job was done.

Jackson wouldn't let them succeed. Piper didn't know it yet, but he was staying glued to her side until this case was solved. His mouth quirked as he thought about their argument last night. She'd fight him on the protection detail. Independent, strong-willed, and challenging. But there was a sweetness to her as well. A vulnerability that she rarely showed. The combination drew him in, made him want to be closer to her. It always had.

She shuffled some papers and then glanced over, catching him looking at her. "You okay?"

Embarrassment heated his cheeks. He'd been staring like a love-sick schoolboy. "I'm fine." Jackson took a swig of water, letting the cool liquid soothe his smoke-damaged throat. "How's your shoulder?"

The corner of her mouth lifted. "It hurts, but don't tell Derek that, or he'll put me on desk duty."

"Ugh. There's nothing worse than piles of paper-work." Ranger Daniel Perez pulled out a chair. Jackson's colleague tossed his white cowboy hat on the table before running a hand through his salt-and-pepper hair. Pushing fifty and divorced, Daniel was dedicated to his job. No kids. No hobbies. He did have a very large and loud extended family, but they were incredibly supportive of his career and never complained when he had to cancel last minute or change plans.

Daniel grinned. "I'm saving my extra paperwork for Cole. He comes off medical leave next week but won't be ready for full duty for another month."

"That's cruel." Jackson grinned back at his friend. "Especially since I'm doing the same."

Daniel laughed, drawing the attention of Ranger Felicity Capshaw. The dark-haired beauty was petite with dainty features, but she was tough enough to flip a suspect over and make him cry for his mama if necessary. Her strength was only superseded by her brains, and Jackson was glad to have her on the task force.

Felicity propped her hands on her hips. "You two have to get in line. I helped Cole rescue Olivia from the stalker, so I get dibs on his help."

"Hold on there." Jackson arched his brows. "I worked that case too. You can't cut ahead of me in line."

"Sure I can." She waved a hand over the piles of paperwork covering the conference room table. "Unless you'd like to spend the next few days interviewing Elena's friends and sifting through her phone records. I'm happy to sit back with my feet up and eat a breakfast burrito." She shrugged, her lips curving up into a smile. "Your choice."

Piper leaned over. "Back off, Barker. She's got you cornered."

Jackson raised his hands in the classic sign of surrender. "I concede. You get dibs on Cole."

The entire group laughed. A moment later, the conference room door opened, and the sheriff strolled in followed by Jackson's boss, Lieutenant Vikki Rodriguez.

The next few minutes were spent getting everyone settled with snacks and beverages.

"Okay, let's get started, people." Derek settled in his chair, then tilted his head one way and then the other, as if his neck was stiff. His dark hair was damp from a recent shower, his uniform clean and pressed, but his expression was grumpy. Jackson could hardly blame him. Within a few days, the town had a murder, a shooting at the sheriff's department, and a bombing in a neighborhood. The media scrutiny was intense. "What did Elena's tablet tell us?"

"She was having an affair with Shawn Kingston." Piper passed around packets she'd prepared for the task meeting. "Text messages, phone calls, and photographs all confirm the relationship. It started a year ago, and according to the messages, ended two weeks before her death."

"Who ended it?" Jackson asked, flipping through the pages. Dozens of texts and phone calls happened between Shawn and Elena. They were flirty but also sometimes intimate. The relationship wasn't a mere fling.

"Elena did. Based on her messages, she was done being a mistress. Shawn was unwilling to end his marriage. That left Elena with no choice."

Piper rose, intending to circle the table to the whiteboard. The window of the conference room had been replaced since the shooting, the bullet holes in the walls patched and the damaged chair removed, but Jackson still had the sudden urge to grab Piper's hand so she'd stay next to him. But that wouldn't be professional. Or reasonable. So he curled his hands into fists to tamp down the impulse.

She used a marker to add dates to the timeline. "Shawn repeatedly attempted to get Elena back. He sent dozens of messages and called her numerous times. Even sent flowers to her house. She deliberately ignored him. Three days later, she was dead."

Silence filled the room. All of them had worked enough cases to know that rejection could turn into deadly obsession. Jackson's stomach soured at the thought of his childhood friend luring Elena to the woods to beat and kill her. "Do we know why Elena went to the nature preserve? Who was she meeting?"

"It's unclear. She received a phone call from an unknown number about an hour before her death. The killer used a burner phone to hide his identity. I've traced the purchase of the phone to a store three counties over. The person paid cash. I attempted to obtain security footage from the store, but it's deleted every three days. Since the phone was purchased five days ago, the footage is gone."

Frustration nipped at Jackson. It would've made things a lot easier if there was security footage of the killer buying the cell phone. He did a quick calculation in his head. "The killer bought the phone two days before Elena was killed."

"Yes." Piper's mouth flattened into a thin line. "This was premeditated. The only communication between our victim and the burner phone was this one call to set up the meeting at the nature preserve."

"If Elena had ignored Shawn's texts and other gestures, why would she agree to meet him?" Daniel asked as he flipped through the pages. "Seems to me, she was purposefully avoiding him. In fact... why call her at all? They worked at the same place. He could've arranged the meeting in person. It would've been a lot easier and untraceable."

Jackson had to admit his fellow ranger had a point. Shawn was clearly upset over the end of his relationship with Elena, but that didn't make him a killer.

"We need to be careful," Derek said, echoing Jackson's thoughts. "I don't want to narrow our investigation to one person. According to several neighbors, Wally Hutchinson threatened Elena openly. He was furious with her for helping his ex move out. He's abusive and aggressive and has been arrested for violence against women in the past."

"Wally's also missing," Felicity added. "No one has seen or heard from him since Wednesday afternoon. I checked with the Watering Hole, which is a bar Wally and his brother frequent. The bartender confirmed both men were there from about noon until 4:30 or so. Then they left with Gerdie."

"All together?" Piper asked. "Todd told us he stayed for a few hours at the bar after Wally left."

"Not according to the bartender. They closed out their tab at 4:32, and he says left right after. All together. I asked for the security footage, but the cameras above the door and the register are broken. The system hasn't worked in two years."

"The meeting between Elena and her killer was set for 5:00." Lieutenant Rodriguez ran a hand over her dark ponytail before tossing the strands over her shoulder. "How far is the bar from the nature preserve?"

"About 15 mins. Wally could've easily driven to the parking lot to meet Elena with time to spare. Did they take separate cars to the bar?"

"No way to know for certain. The parking lot doesn't have cameras."

Jackson mulled that over. "Todd says he met his brother there, but he lied to us about what time he left, so I wouldn't take anything he said as gospel. Did the bartender notice if they came in together?"

"He didn't, but Wally left work around 12:45. It matches the timeline if he drove directly to the bar." Felicity shrugged. "Having said that, Todd's house isn't far from the bar. Wally could've picked up his brother along the way."

"Would Elena have agreed to meet with Wally?" Piper challenged. "Or his brother, Todd. Considering what she knew about Wally—including the fact that he's an abuser and had openly threatened her—I seriously doubt she'd have agreed to meet either of them in a secluded location."

"We don't know what the killer said to her," Daniel argued back. "All we know is there was a phone call."

Felicity nodded. "According to the bartender, Wally was hanging out with a woman for most of the afternoon.

Gerdie James. Apparently, she and Wally go way back and have dated off and on for years. She left with the Hutchinson brothers. It's possible they asked Gerdie to make the call to Elena to arrange the meeting."

Piper nodded. "There are photos of Gerdie and Elena together on social media. They knew each other."

Jackson's worry for the woman deepened. She could've unwittingly helped with the murder. He could easily imagine a scenario where Wally convinced—or threatened—Gerdie to call Elena claiming to have a flat tire or some other kind of car trouble. Based on what they knew about Elena, she would've come to her friend's aid.

"Where's Gerdie?" Derek asked.

"She's missing. Hasn't been seen since leaving the bar with Wally. Right now, there's no way to know if she's willingly with Wally or if she's being held against her will. Or..." Felicity winced. "She's dead."

A dark feeling settled over the group like a heavy cloak. Jackson sent up a prayer for Gerdie's safety. If Wally had killed Elena, there was no telling the horrors he was capable of.

"A BOLO has been issued on Wally's vehicle," Felicity continued. "So far, it hasn't been spotted. We're also interviewing coworkers and neighbors, but no one can tell us where he is. There's not any evidence tying Wally to Elena's murder, so we don't have enough for a search warrant of his residence. Even if we did, it wouldn't help much. He was living at a pay-as-you-go hotel and hasn't paid rent in two weeks. They evicted him on the same day Elena died."

"Could he have been living with his brother?" Lieutenant Rodriguez asked.

"We spoke to the neighbors. No one saw him there, but that doesn't mean much. In that neighborhood, they mind their business. Mrs. Wainwright was the most helpful and she hadn't seen Wally's truck around lately."

Piper shrugged. "Doesn't mean much. If he's late on his rent, he's probably late on his truck payment. He might be hiding the vehicle to prevent them from repossessing it."

Jackson leaned back in his chair. "I tried to interview Todd again after the bombing this afternoon. No one answered the door. His truck and his dog were gone." His jaw tightened. "Whoever set the bomb was close enough to watch as Piper and I entered Elena's house. It was a targeted attack. Todd's house has a clear line of sight. He also knew we were there because we spoke to him before going across the street."

"Todd doesn't have the same criminal record as his brother," Daniel passed out his own packet of papers. "Wally has been in and out of trouble for decades. His charges are extensive and he's bounced in and out of prison. Todd, on the other hand, hasn't been in trouble for years. Not since his twenties. A history of breaking and entering, one charge of domestic violence that was dropped, and a few drug charges that were pled down. Then nothing for almost a decade, until recently. He was arrested last year for possession of marijuana during a routine traffic stop. The charges were later dropped."

"Either of these guys have experience building explosives?" Lieutenant Rodriguez asked.

"Wally spent some time in the military before being dishonorably discharged for assaulting his girlfriend. He didn't work specifically in the bomb-making squad, but he lived with a guy who did. It's possible he picked up a thing or two from his roommate."

"Let's interview the roommate and find out."

Daniel nodded. "On it."

Jackson flipped through Todd's arrest record. "Paul Kingston represented Todd in his recent drug charge. What about Wally?"

"Shawn is listed as his attorney," Felicity said. "It's not surprising, though, right? The Kingstons are well-known criminal defense attorneys."

Jackson nodded absently, but his mind was whirling. "The Kingston Law Firm also represented Marcus, the man who shot at Piper yesterday morning. So far, everyone involved in this case has ties to them. Including Elena."

"What are you suggesting?" Derek asked.

"I'm not entirely sure. It seems far too coincidental that Piper was shot at and then nearly blown up right after Elena's murder. There's no direct evidence to connect these crimes together, but it's the only thing that makes sense. If the killer was merely trying to destroy evidence, he could've blown up Elena's house at any time. He specifically waited for Piper and me to enter. So, let's assume the incidents are all connected for a moment. What do we know about the gun Marcus used? Is it the same one that killed Elena?"

"No. It's connected to a robbery in Houston from five years ago. Store clerk was shot and killed. No suspects." Derek frowned. "Marcus couldn't have committed the crime. He was in county lockup at the time on a disorderly charge."

"Criminals sometimes give weapons to their attorneys, don't they?" Piper asked. "Unless charges were filed, the Kingston Law Firm would have no obligation to hand the weapon over to the prosecution."

"True, but Marcus and the Hutchinson brothers live in the same neighborhood," Derek pointed out. "It's reasonable to assume they knew each other. One of them could have given the gun to Marcus."

Jackson nodded. He studied the whiteboard. A few crime scene photos were tacked up, held in place by magnets. "Elena was beaten before being stabbed. That's a lot of rage. It's personal. And Shawn lied to us about the affair with Elena."

Felicity shrugged. "Maybe he didn't want his wife to find out. Shawn wouldn't be the first person to lie about an affair."

"True, but I offered him a chance to come clean about the affair and I would do everything in my power to keep it quiet. His response was hostile." The reaction didn't sit well. "What if Shawn and Wally are in it together? Shawn could've lured Elena to the parking lot under false pretenses, claiming he needed help, and then killed her. It could explain why Elena's cell was taken by the killer, along with her purse. Shawn didn't want us to uncover the affair they were having. Things got complicated when Elena ran into Piper though. Now Shawn has a detective and a Texas Ranger on his tail."

Derek frowned. "So he hires Wally to do what? Kill you two. That would only put more focus on the case. It makes far more sense that Wally is behind all of this. He kills Elena to get revenge and then targeted Piper because he's worried she saw something and can identify him. It explains why he disappeared after the murder."

"Do Wally and Marcus know each other?" Lieutenant Rodriguez asked.

Piper nodded. "They live in the same neighborhood and went to school together."

"Then I have to agree with Sheriff Martinez. It's a stretch to believe Shawn would hire Wally. We won't ignore the possibility, but without solid evidence, it's unwise to put our focus there. Our primary objective should be finding Wally and Todd. As far as I'm concerned, they're persons of interest in this matter. Has anyone filed a missing person report for Gerdie?"

Felicity nodded. "Her sister did."

"Good. We need to put resources into finding her too."

There was a knock on the conference room door. When Derek barked for the person to enter, a deputy stuck his head in the door. "Sorry to interrupt, sir, but the Kingstons are here to see you. They insist on speaking to you and Ranger Barker about the murder case."

Jackson's brows arched. "They found out we know about the affair."

"Probably." Derek pushed away from the table. "That's okay. I have a few questions of my own. While it's likely these crimes are connected, we don't have solid evidence linking them. For the time being, Elena's murder case is separate from the bombing and yesterday's shooting. Shawn hasn't been cleared from the suspect list. Since he had an affair with Elena, he had motive to want her dead. We need to keep working until we can eliminate him."

"I'll coordinate with Daniel and Felicity about the interviews and evidence we still need to review," Lieutenant Rodriguez said. "I may include another few rangers to the task force since you're short-staffed, sheriff." Her expression darkened. "I don't take kindly to someone coming after a fellow law enforcement officer. It doesn't help when one of my men is getting caught in the crossfire."

The lieutenant was very protective of her team. It was one of the reasons she'd attended the meeting today. No one would get away with threatening someone on Company A. Not on her watch.

Derek gave her a sharp nod. "It's appreciated, Lieutenant." He started for the door. "Jackson, Piper, you're with me."

Jackson rose, collecting his cowboy hat from the table and settling it on his head. Interviewing Shawn again took some mental preparation. He hardened his heart as his gaze swept across the whiteboard. These cases were connected. He was sure of it. Shawn's reaction when he was questioned about Elena was suspicious. Maybe he was covering up his affair, but Jackson had a feeling there was more to it. Shawn could've hired Wally to kill Piper. If nothing else, it would help cover up the true motive for Elena's murder.

Jackson's gaze met Piper's for a moment. The questions rolling through his mind were reflected in her eyes.

Were they about to face off with a killer?

FIFTEEN

The tension in the sheriff's office was thick enough to choke a man.

Jackson stood in the corner of the room. Shawn was seated at a small conference table in the sheriff's office. He attempted to appear in control, but worry lines bracketed his mouth and his shoulders curved inward. Something about his demeanor resembled a dog that'd been beaten down. His wife, Melanie, was seated next to him, but her body leaned away. As if she couldn't stand being so close. Her sunny blond hair hung in waves and she was dressed casually in designer jeans and a lace top. She absently twisted her wedding ring with her thumb.

Standing behind Shawn was his father. Paul Kingston's posture was ramrod straight. His gray hair was cropped short, and he wore an expensive suit tailored to fit his athletic frame perfectly. Looks were very important, and Paul worked out religiously to keep in good health. He was fifty-five but looked a decade younger. His expression was neutral, but Jackson sensed the anger pouring off of him.

"Sheriff, it has come to my attention that you have questions about Shawn's involvement with a receptionist from our law firm." Paul's gaze was sharp enough to cut a man. "We're here to set the record straight. Although why I wasn't given the common courtesy of a heads up before investigators questioned my son, I'll never understand. This entire matter could have been handled quickly."

Paul was furious. Jackson stepped forward to explain that he was in charge of the investigation, but before he could open his mouth, Derek cut him off.

"Paul, I understand this is difficult for your family, but questioning those closest to the victim is standard procedure." Derek's tone brooked no argument. "I won't treat your family any differently than I would any other citizen."

"We'll see how that works out for you when the next election rolls around."

The Kingstons were a wealthy and influential family. If they backed someone else in the next election for sheriff, it would make things difficult for Derek. It didn't surprise Jackson that Paul believed he should be treated with special care. The Kingstons had courted favor with the mayor, the city council, and the sheriff for decades. During Shawn's reckless youth, it had kept him out of trouble.

Apparently, Paul and Shawn were struggling with the idea that they wouldn't be given special dispensation by the sheriff anymore. To his credit, Derek didn't blink at the threat. "You are free to do as you please, Paul." He gave him a relaxed smile. "It's what makes our country so great. That we can choose which leaders we like. In the meantime, I have a murder investigation to run—"

"About that." Paul reached into a leather briefcase and removed a stack of papers, slapping them on Derek's desk. "There are five affidavits from employees who confirm Shawn was at work during the time the victim was killed. He was at the office until well past eight o'clock that night.

Jackson stiffened. If Shawn had an alibi, why hadn't he mentioned it during their first interview?

From the crease of Piper's brow, she was thinking the same thing. She picked up the affidavits and flipped through them. She glanced at Shawn and then at Jackson before handing the papers to Derek. "These appear to be in order."

Paul scoffed. "Of course they are. It's preposterous to believe my son murdered anyone."

"He had a relationship—"

Paul waved off her comment. "Shawn and Melanie have experienced marital troubles for quite some time. That information isn't public knowledge, mind you, but his affair with our receptionist is hardly scandalous."

"Elena," Piper snapped.

"Excuse me?"

"Your receptionist had a name. It's Elena." She turned away from Paul's smirk and focused on Melanie, softening her voice. "Is that true? Did you know about the affair?"

"I did. Shawn and I have been having marital troubles for some time. We've kept it quiet because we aren't sure how we want to proceed. Our children—" A choke cut her off, and tears appeared at the corners of her eyes. "Our children are the most important things to us."

"We've been sleeping in separate bedrooms for a year," Shawn added. "Both of us have had relationships outside of the marriage. For obvious reasons, we've been discreet. The last thing I want is to cause my wife—or my children—embarrassment. People in town would talk if news about my affair became public knowledge."

Jackson spotted a box of tissues on the bookshelf and handed it to Melanie. She delicately removed a few and dabbed at her eyes. "Thank you."

He nodded in silent acknowledgment. Shawn glanced at his wife with concern. She refused to meet his gaze. The interactions were fraught with tension and unspoken conflict. It wasn't hard to see their marriage was on the rocks. Still, there was something about this entire situation that didn't feel right. As if they'd rehearsed their parts. Maybe it was his suspicious nature firing overtime, but Jackson wasn't buying that Melanie knew about the affair before Elena's death.

"I have a few follow-up questions." Jackson returned the tissues to the bookshelf.

"Melanie, dear, why don't you wait outside for us?" Paul's tone was gentle, his expression sympathetic. "There's no need for you to hear anything further."

She quickly rose and scurried from the room like a mouse. The door clicked closed behind her.

Jackson faced Shawn. "We've had time to review Elena's text messages and her phone calls. She broke things off with you about two weeks before she died. Elena was unhappy you wouldn't get a divorce. You persisted in pursuing her, even after things were over. Honestly, I'm confused. If your wife was aware of the affair, and you and Elena were in love, why didn't you simply agree to a divorce?"

Paul placed a meaty hand on Shawn's shoulder and squeezed. "Don't answer that."

Shawn flinched. His hands gripped the arms of the chairs and his jaw clenched, as if he had an answer, but was forbidden from saying it. Jackson knew Shawn's relationship with his dad was fraught with tension. Always had been. Paul expected his orders to be obeyed at all times. The fact that Shawn was a grown man, capable of making his own decisions, didn't matter in the Kingston family. Paul was the patriarch, and his word was law.

He scowled at Jackson. "My son's personal life is not relevant to your murder investigation. He has an alibi for the time Elena was killed." Paul stressed the word Elena, his gaze shooting to Piper briefly before returning to Jackson. "I understand you may be short on suspects, but I will not allow you to rummage around in our private business. Shawn has an alibi for the murder. That's enough to clear him."

Actually it wasn't. The affidavits were from people who worked at the law firm. Jackson wasn't sure if the employees would lie for their boss, but it was possible. Shawn and Paul signed their paychecks. Not to mention there were multiple entrances and exits in the building. Shawn could've slipped out without anyone knowing.

Jackson didn't say any of that though. He didn't want to tip off the Kingstons to the avenues they would be investigating.

Paul's expression hardened. "This matter is resolved. If I find out that anyone has been asking questions or digging into Shawn, I'll sue for defamation." He locked gazes with Derek. "It's in your best interest, as the elected sheriff, to ensure this town is safe. That means protecting all of its citizens in every way. I don't expect my family's name to be dragged through the mud."

With those parting words, Paul and Shawn left.

Piper blew out a breath as she watched the Kingstons hurry across the bullpen through the glass walls of the office. "Anyone else feel like we were being handled?"

"Oh yeah." Jackson rocked back on the heels of his boots. "I suspect Shawn told Paul and his wife about the affair following our first interview. This was damage control."

"An effective one." Derek picked up the affidavits. "I'll have deputies individually question these individuals, but if their statements hold up, it appears Shawn had an alibi for the time Elena was killed."

"That doesn't preclude him from hiring Wally to do his dirty work." Jackson was more convinced Shawn was neck-deep in this somehow. He hated the thought. Shawn was an old friend, but his handling of the matter only reinforced the idea that he had something to hide. And Jackson wasn't convinced it was an affair.

Derek sighed. "I don't like what just happened any more than you do, but we don't have any proof that Shawn hired Wally. We have to follow the evidence, and right now, our primary suspect is Wally. If Shawn hired him, then we'll find proof of it during the investigation."

Jackson reluctantly nodded. Derek was right. Suspicion and gut instinct didn't go very far in a courtroom. Everything they'd uncovered thus far pointed to Wally. He rubbed his forehead. A headache was brewing along his temples. Maybe he was too close to this investigation. With Piper's life being threatened, Jackson had to admit he might not be seeing things clearly.

"You two take the rest of the afternoon off," Derek said. "Neither of you can move without wincing. We'll reconvene in the morning and see where the investigation is." He pegged Piper with a stern look. "Rest, Detective Jensen. That's an order. Don't even look at this case file until tomorrow morning."

She wrinkled her nose. "I can read over evidence reports—"

"No. I've got Ranger Perez and Ranger Capshaw in the conference room to do that. Plus, more rangers are showing up tomorrow." Worry darkened his brown eyes until they were almost black. "I'll have extra patrols go by your house, Piper, and once the night shift starts, someone will be stationed on your street. Use caution." His gaze shifted between Jackson and Piper. "Both of you. I'm not sure how the bombing, the shooting, and Elena's murder fit together yet, but until we know more... assume you're in danger."

SIXTEEN

Piper absently stroked Moxie's head while she studied Wally Hutchinson's most recent arrest photo.

It was from a year ago. He'd been charged with domestic violence, but the charges were later dropped when the victim refused to testify. That wasn't uncommon unfortunately. What was frightening was that the woman he assaulted was Gerdie James, the same one who was now missing. Piper's stomach swirled with anxiety for the young woman. Deputies were interviewing her friends, but so far, no one had heard from her or had the slightest clue where she was. Todd also hadn't returned to his house, and none of Wally's friends or coworkers knew where he was.

The resemblance between the Hutchinson brothers was obvious. They had the same slope to their nose, thin lips, and cleft chin. However, unlike Todd's receding hairline, Wally's dark hair was thick and curly. His face, square and weathered, was marked by deep-set eyes under bushy eyebrows. His mouth was a thin slash. He was harder looking. Meaner. Based on his arrest record, he'd spent most of his adult life in and out of prison.

Something about him unsettled Piper. Wally had lived in her neighborhood while she was a child. It was probable they'd crossed paths, but she had no recollection of him.

She pushed aside his arrest photo and studied Gerdie's picture. It'd been taken from a social media site. She was young—barely twenty-two—with delicate features, long blonde hair, and bright blue eyes. Her smile was tight and there was a haunted look about her.

"You okay, baby girl?"

Grandma Mary's voice shocked Piper out of her thoughts. She jumped slightly and then placed a hand over her racing heart. "You scared me."

"Sorry." Grandma Mary stood close by in soft-soled shoes. Her coat was slung over her arm, purse on her shoulder. "I called your name a few times, but you didn't answer."

"I was lost in thought."

Grandma Mary's expression grew sympathetic. "I can imagine." She glanced at Gerdie's photograph on the kitchen table and sighed. "Poor girl. She never had it easy."

"You know her?"

"She stayed with me for a month or two right after her momma died. She went to live with her grandmother shortly after that, but I don't think it was a happy household. Her grandpappy was as mean as her daddy.

Drinkers, the whole lot of them." A pained look entered her eyes. "Do you think she's okay?"

"I don't know. We believe she's with Wally Hutchinson." Piper pulled his arrest photo closer for Grandma Mary to see. She'd grown up in Rock Fort and knew everyone. Her observations weren't evidence, but it could help lead them in a new direction. "What do you know about him?"

"He's too much like his daddy. There's something about a person... they have a look of cruelty about them. Wally is one of those. He takes pleasure in hurting others." Mary's brow crinkled. "I had an altercation with him once. We were in the grocery store, and he was following us around. I didn't like the way he was watching you."

"When was this? I don't remember it."

"You were pretty young. Maybe thirteen. It was the second or third time you came to live with me. Anyway, I got the store manager involved, and the police were called. Wally was given a warning. He never did it again, but that incident sticks out in my mind. There was something about him... like he was on the hunt. It always bothered me."

A shiver raced down Piper's spine. She didn't remember the incident in the grocery store at all, but there were large sections of her childhood she couldn't recall. It was a trauma response. Was the grocery store incident the only run-in she'd had with Wally? Or were there more and she couldn't remember?

It would explain why she had such a visceral negative reaction to Wally.

"There's a storm coming." Grandma Mary kissed the top of Piper's head. "I'd best get these old bones home before the rain starts." Her lips lifted in a smile. "And you should head into the living room. Jackson is helping Finn with the piano piece for church on Sunday. It's sweet to watch."

Tonight, Jackson had slipped into their family dynamic as easily as if he'd been there for years. He'd colored with Emma, helped Mary straighten up the living room, and even played with Moxie outside in the yard while Piper prepared ice cream sundaes. Now he was tutoring Finn on the piano. The notes flowed smoothly and sounded more confident than they had the day before.

Curiosity drew her to the living room. Ava rested on the sofa, her injured leg propped up on an ottoman. Curled up at her side was Emma. Dark hair damp from a shower and dressed in pajamas, she was ready for bed. The music must've brought her back downstairs. Moxie trotted in behind Piper and hopped up on the couch. He lay close to Emma, his ears pitched forward.

Seated at the piano bench was Finn. His fingers flew over the keys as the piece picked up. Jackson stood nearby, watching every movement with intensity, and then he cheered silently when Finn executed a specific part flawlessly. He completed the piece, the last note of music fading, and then the entire room burst into applause.

Finn sat back with a satisfied grin. "I did it! Finally."

"It was beautiful!" Ava's eyes were full of pride and joy. "Pastor Mike will be overjoyed and the church congregation will love it."

"I couldn't have done it without Jackson's help." Finn closed the sheets of music and tossed Jackson a grateful look. "Your advice on the finger placement made all the difference. Thank you."

Jackson clapped Finn on the shoulder. "My suggestions were minor tweaks. You did all the hard work. I'm impressed by your talent and dedication. That piece isn't easy, but you kept at it until it was right."

Finn seemed to grow inches taller under Jackson's praise. Ava and Piper complimented him often, but somehow, Jackson's words landed differently. Finn needed the guidance of a male role model. He had his baseball coach and Pastor Mike, but maybe that wasn't enough? Or perhaps it was Jackson. He had this special something... it wasn't charm or charisma... it was genuineness. A sincerity in his words that reached right inside and knocked down every wall around a person's heart.

"I'm sorry to say it, kiddos, but it's bedtime." Ava struggled to her feet, waving off Piper's help. From the way her mouth flattened, she was in pain but unwilling to admit it. Stubborn at every turn. "Jackson, thank you for everything."

Her tone was warm with affection. Ava had always liked Jackson, but his actions since arriving back in town had firmly entrenched her in his camp. She shot a look toward Piper that was loaded with instructions and warnings. The meaning couldn't have been more clear if her sister had shouted the words: He's perfect. Don't screw it up.

Piper ignored Ava's pointed gaze and hugged Emma. The little girl kissed Piper's cheek.

Finn gave Jackson a fist bump. "Night."

Jackson's grin widened. "See you tomorrow."

Emma rushed him, her little arms barely able to encircle half his waist. Jackson picked her up and whirled her around like she was a doll. Peals of laughter filled the room, along with Moxie's barking. The lab attempted to jump on Jackson in order to join in the fun.

Piper snagged his collar before his nails accidentally caught on Emma. "Cool it, Moxie."

He licked her hand, his dark brown eyes dancing with mischief, but he obeyed by sitting on his rump. She gave him a few scratches behind the ear and then he ran off to join Ava and the kids as they made their way upstairs. Suddenly, Piper and Jackson were alone.

He slid onto the piano bench and patted the cushion in invitation.

She joined him. Her heart fluttered as their shoulders brushed. "You made Finn's night. He's been working on that piece for weeks."

"I was happy to do it. Your family is wonderful. I know you and Ava have had your struggles, but the love and happiness you give those kids... it's a joy to be around."

Tears sprang to Piper's eyes, catching her off-guard. Jackson's compliment touched her in a place she hadn't known was wounded and hurting. She often worried about her capacity to love. Growing up in chaos and conflict, it was hard to trust that she would ever be good enough. That notion had been reinforced when townsfolk whispered behind her back or kids called her bad names on the playground.

Jackson saw her differently. He always had. It was intoxicating and terrifying all at once.

His fingers touched the keys, releasing a sweet melody Piper instantly recognized. Her song. The one Jackson had composed during their summer romance all those years ago. Memories flooded her mind, making her heart ache in a way she hadn't known was possible. The heat of Jackson's body seeped through the sleeve of her shirt where their shoulders touched. Piper was mesmerized by the way his strong hands danced over the keys. Those same hands had protected her today. Carried her away from the smoke and the fire to safety. She'd always known he was brave, but today proved it.

The last note lingered in the air. Jackson turned toward Piper and her gaze instinctively lifted to his. Her breath hitched. Desire shimmered in the depths of his green eyes, a yearning that matched the one in her heart. Butterflies once again took flight in her stomach. She reached up and gently touched his face. The rough edges of his whiskers scraped against the pads of her fingers.

Jackson's gaze dropped to her mouth. She knew it was a mistake but couldn't help herself. He'd always been her weakness.

Piper leaned closer in silent invitation, and when his

mouth brushed against hers, the intensity of emotion shooting through her took over. No other man had ever affected her this way. It didn't matter that it'd been ten years since they last dated. Or that they'd been around each other for only three days. The embers of their romance lingered and clearly it didn't take much to reignite them. Resisting was impossible.

Piper threaded her fingers through the soft strands at the nape of his neck. Jackson deepened the kiss, his passion and gentleness sweeping her away.

When the embrace ended, she was breathless. Jackson rested his forehead against hers. His hands cupped the sides of her face, her pulse pounding against his thumbs. "I was terrified when that bomb went off. I thought…"

"Me too." Worry seeped into the warmth his kisses had left. Piper pulled back slightly. "But we can't simply pick up where we left off."

"I don't expect us to, but I would like for us to finally be honest with each other." He touched her cheek. "Why, sweetheart? Why did you leave without talking to me first?"

Fear gripped her. It stiffened her muscles and iced her blood, washing away any warmth from his touch. Piper pulled back more. She touched her slightly swollen lips. What had she just done?

She rose from the piano bench. Distance. She needed distance from him. Blindly, she faced the window overlooking the backyard. Darkness stretched beyond the gleam of the porch light. Trees rippled in the wind, and farther away, lightning flashed. A storm was brewing. It matched the whipping emotions whirling through her.

She'd left to protect him. Jackson deserved so much better than her. It was true before the attack, but after... it was undeniable. Her PTSD was overwhelming. No one could touch her. She wanted to cry and hide under the covers. It took every ounce of will to keep drawing in a breath.

She'd been weak. Broken. And she'd hated it.

Piper was better now, but she was also changed. The attack taught her to be cautious about reaching too high. Despite her childhood, she'd studied hard and gotten into college. Fallen in love with Jackson. Just as she thought her life was finally going in the right direction...

It'd all come crashing down.

God loved her. Piper knew that with every ounce of her being, but she also understood that trouble followed her. She was damaged. It wasn't fair to drag Jackson into that mess. They weren't meant to be, no matter how much she wished otherwise.

"We were young, Jackson. There were so many differences between us. What more can I say?"

The words were hollow in the aftermath of that passionate kiss, but she couldn't tell him the truth. Jackson was honorable and brave and beyond loyal. He'd argue with her reasons, but it wouldn't change the underlying truth.

Silence stretched out. Piper felt rather than heard Jackson come up behind her. She didn't dare look at him.

"Yes, we were young, but we also loved each other."

He took a deep breath and let it out slowly. "Being apart made it easy to believe that what existed between us was fleeting. Just a summer romance that ended abruptly. Until I saw you again. Until that kiss."

She closed her eyes, wanting to shut out his words. "We shouldn't have—"

"Don't. Please don't tell me you regret it because I know it's not true."

No, she didn't regret it. How could she? It was a stolen moment that she'd carry with her for the rest of her life. Piper swallowed hard. "It wasn't smart."

She whirled away from the window, seeking distance once again. Piper couldn't think with him near. "We're working together to find a killer. This case is complicated. Letting our stuff impede the investigation is a disservice to Elena."

"Neither of us would ever do that, and you know it." His jaw tightened as he reached for her. "Don't push me away, Piper. I deserve better than that."

He did, but she didn't know how to move beyond her fear and limitations.

Piper's cell phone rang, interrupting their conversation. She sucked in a breath and pulled the device from her back pocket. It was Derek. Shock quickly followed by a bolt of worry. She answered. "What's wrong?"

"There's another victim."

SEVENTEEN

Jackson's headlights cut through the darkness. Rain battered against his windshield. Thick woods lined either side of the lonely, two-lane country road. In the passenger seat beside him, Piper was pale. Her mouth firmed into a hard line, and one hand gripped the door handle. They hadn't said a word since getting in the SUV. By unspoken agreement, they'd put their personal conversation aside to focus on the horrible task ahead.

He was hurt though. The kiss they'd shared... it was like Jackson had been wearing foggy glasses, and in an instant, he could suddenly see clearly. What existed between them wasn't a faded teenage love or a figment of their imaginations. It was real. Deep. Powerful. It was a bond that couldn't be explained rationally.

On one hand, it was a relief. Jackson could finally understand why he hadn't been able to forget her. Or move on. He'd tried. Dated some wonderful women with amazing qualities, but somewhere in the back of his mind, Piper lingered like a ghost he'd never been able to get rid of. So, yes, it was a relief to realize he wasn't a commitment-phobe. Those woman, as great as they were, weren't right for him.

Unfortunately, Piper's reaction left him frustrated. Worse, Jackson felt alone. Alone in his feelings and alone in his desire to make their relationship work. Once again, she'd rejected and distanced herself from him. Jackson knew she cared about him. For a long time after she'd left, he'd questioned that, but after the kiss they'd shared, there was no doubt.

Nothing made sense. How could she ice him out so easily? Maybe Piper cared, but not to the same degree as he did. Or maybe it was just easier for her to shut down because of her childhood. Either way, the result was the same. Jackson was left struggling and uncertain. Emotions he abhorred.

God, I'm lost. I don't know what to do.

Even now, Jackson wanted to reach across the distance between them and take her hand. Comfort her. Piper was distressed, and the tension pouring from her was nearly palpable. But he didn't give in to the urge. In times of distress, she'd resisted any compassion.

The GPS indicated a turn up ahead, so Jackson eased up on the gas. Darkness pressed in, made worse by the raging thunderstorm, and he nearly missed the faint break in the trees.

"This isn't anywhere close to where Elena was found." Piper's voice was hollow. "We're on the opposite side of the nature preserve. This area is commonly used by families and other visitors." She gestured to another road, this one bigger, leading to the west. "The information center is up there, near the main entrance."

"Did Derek say how the victim was found?"

"A set of hikers found her on a commonly used trail. It doesn't seem like the killer attempted to hide the body."

The road narrowed, winding its way through the nature preserve. His tires rumbled as they crossed a rustic wooden bridge. Down below, the river was a dark slice through the trees. Another turn and they were in a parking lot full of official state and county vehicles. Red and blue lights strobed across the asphalt.

Jackson parked. Crisp air and raindrops whipped across his face when he opened the driver's side door. He unfurled his umbrella. Lightning flashed, followed by a low rumble of thunder. The storm was far from over. It would wreak havoc on the crime scene. The investigators would do everything possible to preserve the evidence, but it was a fact that some would be destroyed by the rain.

Piper joined him, tucked under her own umbrella, and together, they made their way across the parking lot to the cordoned-off area. Derek spotted them from his place under a portable canopy on a nearby trail. He waved them forward. As Jackson drew closer, the victim came into view. His heart sank.

Piper gasped. "That's Gerdie."

The young woman was sprawled on the dirt trail as if she'd fallen. She was wearing jeans and a T-shirt, the same clothes she'd been wearing at the bar, but now they were stained with mud and blood. Her face was battered and bruised. Someone had beaten her.

"Two gunshot wounds, likely to the back, judging from the exit and entrance wounds." Derek looked mad enough to spit nails. "The coroner will have to confirm, of course, but from what I can gather, the killer shot her as she was running away."

Jackson felt his own temper rise. "Wally?"

"He was the last one seen with her. She's been beaten, like Elena was, before being shot. Her body was left in the nature preserve. The M.O. is similar enough to believe we're looking at the same killer."

"He shot her twice." Piper's voice was hollow. "This time he made sure she was dead."

"Yes."

"Do we have a time of death?" Jackson asked.

The coroner's assistant glanced up from where she was bagging Gerdie's hands to preserve any evidence under her fingernails. "She's not in full rigor, so less than twelve hours. Based on her liver temperature, I'm guessing sometime well before that, say in the last six hours or so."

Derek nodded. "The hikers who found her entered the trail at four and then exited using the same path around seven. My guess is, the killer brought her sometime between four and seven. Probably right before the storm."

Jackson did a quick calculation. "So around six. Risky, but calculated. He was hoping the storm would cover his tracks and destroy any evidence. He probably intended for her to be found tomorrow morning, or maybe the day after."

"That's what I think too." Derek glanced at the sky. "It'll be raining off and on for the next two days. Few hikers would venture out in this weather." He gestured to the parking lot. "He brought her here, walked her up the path, and likely told her to run."

"You think he beat her someplace else?"

"Bruises are in layers." The coroner's assistant piped up. "Looks like she was beaten over the course of a couple of days."

Piper growled. "Wally and Gerdie left the bar on Wednesday. That means he held her, and beat her, for two days." She gripped her folded umbrella with enough force to cause her knuckles to whiten. "Wally must've used Gerdie to lure Elena to the woods. It would be difficult to control both women, so maybe he left Gerdie tied up in the car while he killed Elena in the field. Then he kept Gerdie somewhere and continued to beat her until it stopped being fun. Finally, he brings her here. He tells Gerdie to run, and when she does, shoots her in the back twice."

Jackson's stomach swirled as a fresh wave of anger crashed over him. The terror Gerdie had suffered... "We need to find Wally Hutchinson. Based on these two murders, he's likely to kill again."

Piper's cell phone rang. She pulled it from her back pocket and her eyes widened. She tilted the phone so Jackson could view the screen. "Isn't that the same number as the burner phone? The one the killer used to call Elena?"

He nodded, shock sending a shiver of apprehension down his spine.

"Answer it," Derek ordered. "Put the call on speaker."

Piper did as her boss said. The three of them huddled together. Derek was texting on his own device, likely asking headquarters to trace the call. If Piper kept the killer on long enough, they could get a location based on the cell towers the burner phone pinged off.

"Hello, Piper. It's been a long time since we last saw each other."

The words came out distorted, as if the caller was using a voice modulator. For some reason, that only made the call creepier. Jackson scanned the nearby area, searching for any sign of the killer. The trees were thick, and with the storm still raging, it was difficult to discern anything in the dark.

Was he close by? Could he see them?

"Who is this?" Piper's tone was sharp and author-itative.

"Oh, that hurts. You don't remember me? I find that hard to believe after the special moments we shared." Even with the voice modulator, his pitch turned hard and mean. "I taught you a lesson about men, you stupid cow. You were so haughty. Thought you were better than the rest of us. I had to show you with my fists just how weak you actually were. Too bad I didn't put a bullet through you like I did with Gerdie, but there's always next time."

With a sudden jolt, Jackson realized just what the killer was alluding to.

The attack. He was responsible for beating and nearly shooting Piper ten years ago.

Jackson balled his hands into fists as a rage unlike any he'd ever experienced coursed through his veins. It took all his self-control to resist ripping the phone away from Piper and telling the man on the other end just what he was going to do to him.

She gritted her teeth. "You're lying, Wally."

"This isn't Wally. I've got you chasing your tail, don't I, Piper?"

Jackson frowned. The caller could be lying, saying he wasn't Wally when he actually was. Then again, there were so many layers to this case, nothing could be what it seemed. Wally could be stone-cold dead, just like Gerdie.

Piper gripped the phone. "The man who attacked me is dead."

Laughter came from the speaker. "Lionel Islip was a weakling and a coward. He barely had the nerve to break into people's houses. You think he was powerful enough to take you down? No, you needed a real man to teach you how the world works."

Her complexion paled. She swayed. Jackson wrapped an arm around her waist to prevent her from collapsing. He would've also taken the phone from her hand, but Piper jerked it away from him. "Prove you're telling the truth."

"Your hair was in a braid, the kitchen floor was

yellow with a green floral design, and when I approached, you were putting milk in the fridge."

Jackson's gaze shot to Derek. The sheriff's eyes were wide, his teeth bared. Based on his reaction, those details were true.

"I ripped off your necklace," the killer continued. "Gave that to Lionel. I wasn't ready for anyone to know who I truly was."

Bright red spots appeared on Piper's cheeks. She shook. "I'm going to hunt you to the ends of the earth, and when I catch you, you're going to wish you'd never met me."

He laughed again. "Not if I catch you first. See you soon, Piper."

EIGHTEEN

Weak morning sunshine streamed through the curtains in Piper's bedroom, barely breaking through the overcast day. A steady beat thrummed against the window. The rain had lightened up since last night but was far from over. More storms were predicted for this afternoon.

Piper buried herself deeper in the covers. Several layers of thick blankets were piled on top of her comforter, but it didn't erase the chill in her bones. Her eyes felt gritty and sore from not sleeping. After coming home from the crime scene, she'd lain awake in bed, her mind twisting and turning and unable to settle. Not even prayer had soothed her raw nerves. And every time she started drifting off to sleep, her thoughts would return to the phone call. The killer's words replayed on a loop.

Your hair was in a braid, the kitchen floor was yellow with a green floral design, and when I approached, you were putting milk in the fridge.

All of that was true. The last detail wasn't common knowledge. Piper had told Derek, but he hadn't included it in the official report. Some things were held back so investigators could identify the right suspect through questioning when one was arrested. Lionel never confessed. He'd pulled a gun on the police when they arrived to arrest him and was killed in the subsequent shootout.

For the last ten years, Piper believed her attacker was dead. That she was safe. It was over.

Instead, he'd been out there. Free to brutalize other women.

Free to kill.

She tossed the covers off and swung her legs over the bed. It was tempting to hide out. Jackson and Derek could work the case. They were capable and smart investigators who wouldn't stop until the perpetrator was caught. No one would blame her for removing herself from the case. She didn't have to keep going.

She could leave.

Piper had done it before. In fact, her instincts were to run. Get in her car and drive until she ran out of gas or the wheels of her truck fell off. Either that or hide under these covers until the case was solved. The whispers of self-preservation and protection were strong. It took a lot of strength to push them aside.

Piper wasn't a terrified eighteen-year-old. She was a law enforcement officer who'd taken an oath to protect and serve. Running away hadn't solved anything, and hiding out would only reinforce the notion that she was weak. Piper refused to be broken. No one—not even the threats of a homicidal maniac—would stop her from finishing what she'd started. Elena and Gerdie deserved justice. So did she.

It was time to get it.

She rushed through her morning routine. The doors in the hallway were all closed. Her sister and the kids were still sleeping, not surprising since it was dawn on a Saturday morning. A patrol unit was stationed outside the house and Jackson had insisted on spending the night on the couch. One of the first things that needed to be addressed was her family's safety. The killer seemed fixated on Piper, but she was smart enough to know, a desperate man might hurt those closest to her.

The scent of coffee tickled her senses as she hit the last step on the stairs. Voices filtered from the kitchen. Male. Piper rounded the corner and found Jackson seated at the table with two other men. Texas Rangers, judging from the badges pinned to their shirts.

He rose. "Good morning. Piper, I'd like to introduce you to Ranger Cole Donnelly and Ranger Weston Donovan. Both of them work with me in Company A."

Cole had short blonde hair and when he extended his right hand for her to shake, winced slightly. "Pleasure to meet you, Detective Jensen."

"Piper, please." She smiled. "I've heard a lot about you, Ranger Donnelly, starting with the fact that you were shot in the line of duty. How's your recovery?"

"Slower than I'd like, thanks."

Weston rolled his eyes. "Don't listen to him. He's such a whiner. Cole acts like he's the only one in our group who's been shot." His tone was teasing, and it was obvious he was good-naturedly picking on his teammate. Weston was built like a tank and towered over Piper. When they shook hands, his grip was firm but not crushing, and his smile warm. "Nice to meet you. Pardon our invasion into your home, but Jackson thought it was better to meet here than at the sheriff's department."

"Weston and Cole have volunteered to protect Ava and the kids until the case is solved," Jackson explained.

Piper's mouth dropped open. "But—"

"But nothing." Weston waved off her protest. "Cole is practically useless these days. He's still on medical leave. And I'm technically on vacation." His chest puffed out. "My wife, Avery, gave birth to our gorgeous daughter last week. I took some time off to be with them, but yesterday, her sister and grandmother arrived to help. Now there are three women fluttering around my sweet daughter, and I'll be lucky to catch sight of her, let alone hold her."

Piper laughed. "Do you have a picture of your daughter?"

Cole rolled his eyes. "He has hundreds. I've never seen so many photos of a newborn in my whole life."

"That's because she's the most beautiful girl in the world." Weston whipped out his cell phone and opened his photos app before turning the screen toward Piper. "Her name is Charlotte."

On screen was one of the cutest babies Piper had ever seen. Wispy dark curls framed a round face with a perfect button nose and a rosebud mouth. Charlotte was nestled in a pink blanket decorated with elephants. Piper smiled. "She is gorgeous. Congratulations." She pointed to the woman holding the infant. "Is that your wife?"

"Yes. Avery. She's the chief of police for Harrison University." Weston clapped Jackson on the back. "Get this lump to invite you to one of our BBQs. I'm sure everyone would love to meet you, including my wife."

"Aunt Piper."

The tiny voice was filled with nerves. Piper turned to find Emma standing in the doorway, still in her pajamas, a scared look on her face. The little girl's gaze shot from one man to the next.

Heart squeezed tight, Piper scooped up Emma into her arms. The little girl buried her face in her shoulder. Emma's breath was hot against her neck. It must've been unnerving to find the kitchen full of strangers. Emma was an outgoing child, but like everyone, she had her limits. "Don't be frightened. These men are Mr. Jackson's friends. This is Mr. Cole and Mr. Weston."

Emma peeked out from her hiding place.

The guys waved at her, and Weston pulled a silly face, which elicited a round of giggles from the kindergartener. Within minutes, Emma was plying the two newcomers with questions. Piper cracked eggs while Jackson chopped veggies for the omelets. Fresh coffee brewed, and along the way, someone turned on the radio.

Gospel music filled the kitchen, punctuated by the low murmur of male voices and Emma's frequent giggles.

Jackson set a full mug of coffee on the counter next to Piper. "You look like you need this."

"That obvious, huh?" She whisked the eggs with one hand while grabbing the coffee with the other. Caffeine was a must if she was going to get through the day. "I didn't sleep much."

"Who could after what happened last night?"

She glanced over her shoulder. Piper's heart melted at the sight of the two rangers teaching Emma how to make shadow animals. Then she focused back on Jackson. Butterflies fluttered in her stomach. He hadn't shaved yet, and the whiskers shadowing his chin accented the curve of his lips and the deep green color of his eyes.

Maybe it was tiredness. Or perhaps her heart couldn't forget the passionate kiss they'd shared before the night turned horribly wrong. Whatever it was, Piper gave into the urge to lean forward and brush a kiss across his gorgeous lips. "Thank you for arranging protection for my family. Weston and Cole are great."

His lips curved into a smile, and he brushed a strand of hair from her cheek. "You don't need to thank me. I care about Ava and the kids. I don't want anything to happen to them. Or you, for that matter." His expression darkened as worry filled his eyes. "What are the chances I can talk you into hiding out while we catch whoever is behind this?"

She hesitated and then pulled away under the guise

of pouring the eggs into the frying pan. "I can't. This is my job, Jackson. I have to see it through."

He sighed. "That's what I thought."

"Good morning, everyone." Ava limped in, a smile brightening her face. "I didn't know we were having a party this morning."

"Mommy, look!" Emma shouted. "I can make a dog!"

Piper laughed and introduced her sister to Weston and Cole. A few minutes later, Finn joined them. The kitchen overflowed with conversation, and once breakfast was ready, they all joined hands to pray. It felt as natural as breathing. Piper didn't trust easily. Neither did her sister. But there was something about the men on Jackson's team that broke through their embedded mistrust. It was a shared faith, yes, but it went deeper than that. Cole and Weston were kind and spoke lovingly of their wives and family. Their dedication to the people they cared about, including Jackson, shone through.

She could trust these men with her family. They'd do everything to keep them safe.

The doorbell pealed. Jackson, along with the other rangers, rose immediately.

Piper's phone beeped with a text. She glanced at the screen. "Stand down, gentlemen. It's the sheriff." She strolled from the kitchen and crossed to the front door, but before opening it, confirmed Derek was standing on the porch. He looked terrible. His uniform was wrinkled and there were circles dark enough to count as bruises under his eyes.

She wasn't the only one who hadn't gotten any sleep.

"Derek, come in." She instantly recognized the stiffness in his posture and the concern written on his features. Her pulse picked up. "What is it? Has there been another murder?"

"No, but we need to have the task force meeting here. I think there's a leak in my department." He gestured to the television. "Turn on the news."

NINETEEN

Jackson adjusted the volume on the television as a news reporter came on. She was in the parking lot of the nature preserve, close to where Gerdie's body had been found.

"This is the second woman found murdered in a week." The reporter's expression was appropriately somber, but there was a gleam of excitement in her eyes, as though she was about to reveal a giant secret. "Both victims were beaten and shot, indicating we're looking at the same killer. Sheriff Derek Martinez has been slow to provide updates. Sources have linked these two murders to an attack from ten years ago. A young woman was beaten and nearly shot in her home."

She glanced down at the notes in her hand. "The victim in that earlier attack has been identified as Detective Piper Jensen. She now works for the Rock Fort Sheriff's Department."

Piper inhaled sharply. She sat on the arm of the couch. Spots of color appeared in her cheeks, and although she said nothing, Jackson knew she was deeply upset. Ten years ago, after the assault, she'd been bombarded with questions and comments from towns-folk. Some had been genuine and kind, others nosy and bordering victim shaming. For someone who shied away from attention, both were emotionally and mentally exhausting.

"If this is true," the reporter continued, "then it's concerning that our sheriff is refusing to answer questions. Do we have a serial killer on the loose in Rock Fort? I intended to ask at the press conference scheduled for noon today."

The shot flipped back to the anchors in the studio, and a different story followed. Jackson flipped off the television and nearly threw the remote down on the coffee table. "That news story has Paul Kingston's dirty fingerprints all over it."

Derek nodded. "I've long suspected he was being fed information from my department. Since I took over as sheriff last year, I've done my best to plug the leaks. Clearly, I haven't been successful."

Ava wrapped an arm around her sister's shoulders in silent comfort. Weston and Cole sat on the couch. Both looked furious. Footsteps upstairs punctuated the kids' movements. Finn and Emma were playing in their rooms.

Derek focused on Ava and Piper. "I'm so sorry."

Piper waved off his apology. "This isn't your fault."

Ava nodded in agreement and offered him a smile. "We've been the subject of town gossip more than once and survived." She squeezed Piper's shoulders. "I should go upstairs and talk to Emma and Finn. Some people will shamefully ask them questions. I don't want them to be surprised."

Derek winced. He removed his cowboy hat and ran his hands through the mussed strands, making them stand on end. "Ava…"

"Don't you dare start beating yourself up, Derek. None of this is your fault." She limped across the room and briefly touched his arm with her hand. "I'll take care of the kids. You keep my sister safe and catch this killer."

The doorbell rang. Jackson strolled across the living room to answer it.

Grandma Mary breezed inside the moment the door opened, enveloping him in a hug. "I saw the news story. How are my girls?"

"Hanging in there. But they're upset."

She nodded and then patted his cheek. "You also look upset." She gave him another motherly hug. "When things are bleak, it can be hard to rely on your faith, but keep praying. God is listening. He will ease the burdens in your heart and find some way to bring goodness from these tragedies."

"Thank you, Grandma Mary. I needed to hear that."

"Of course, child." She released him. "You're a good man, Jackson Barker. Always have been. Piper became tough out of necessity, but no one was made to walk this earth alone. It might take her some time, but she'll figure that out." Her gaze drifted to Ava and Derek. "So will Ava."

He sighed. "I hope you're right."

Jackson was about to close the front door when he spotted several members of the ranger team heading up the walkway. Felicity and Daniel were accompanied by Luke Tatum, Grady West, and Bennett Knox. Trailing the group was Lieutenant Vikki Rodriguez, the commander of Company A, and Bennett's wife, Emilia. Emilia worked for the state police as a criminal profiler.

All of them greeted Jackson with a hug or a handshake. Grady paused and lifted the bakery box in his hands. "We brought treats. I also wanted to let you know Tara sent out messages in the prayer group."

Tara was Grady's wife and often initiated the group's social events. All the rangers' wives, girlfriends, and fiancées were close thanks to Tara's leadership. Jackson often wondered how she made time for it all with her busy medical practice and two young children, but she always seemed happy to organize the get-togethers.

"Thanks, Grady. The way this case is going, we need all the prayers we can get."

"We'll catch this guy." Grady patted him on the back. "Don't you worry."

His colleague's words were confident. Relief unfurled as Jackson realized the entire living room was full of topnotch investigators. He sent up a silent prayer to the Lord, giving thanks for his teammates. They were more than friends and colleagues. They were family.

Jackson settled on the couch next to Piper. She leaned closer to him until they were shoulder to shoulder. He was tempted to wrap his arm around her, but that wouldn't be professional. Grandma Mary and Ava quickly went upstairs to talk to the children.

"We've all reviewed the reports and the evidence," Luke said, opening the bakery box. Assorted pastries rested inside. He then tossed napkins down next to trays of takeaway coffee. It was rare the team met without food. "From the looks of things, our number one suspect is Wally Hutchinson. Where are we on locating him?"

"His friends and family have been interviewed multiple times, but no one is telling us much." Derek took a long sip of his coffee. "Todd Hutchinson, his younger brother, is also missing and has been since the bombing at Elena's house. We don't have any evidence directly linking him to the murders or the bombing, so I can't obtain a search warrant for his house."

"What about Kylie Reynolds?" Jackson asked. As an ex-girlfriend and the mother of Wally's child, Kylie might know a lot of helpful information.

"She and her daughter have been placed in protective custody, since there's a possibility Wally may target her next. Kylie's been forthcoming with what she knows, but it's not much." Felicity rolled her eyes. Her hair was braided and hung down her back. "This isn't a surprise, but apparently Wally doesn't think too highly of women. He kept a lot of secrets from Kylie."

"She said Todd and Wally were close but didn't always get along," Daniel added. He was uncharacteristically sporting a five-o'clock shadow, the whiskers a mix of brown and gray. "But they're very loyal to each other. Hurt one and you'll tussle with them both."

"So it's possible Wally and his brother are hiding out together." Jackson frowned. "Still he transported Gerdie somehow. Why hasn't his car been spotted? We have a BOLO on it."

"He could've changed out the license plates with stolen ones," Weston suggested. "Criminals like Wally would know to do that to avoid detection. He could even be driving a stolen car. We've sent Wally's photo and information to every law enforcement agency in the state, labeling him as a person of interest."

"I'm also going to share his information in the press conference, letting everyone know, including Wally, that we need to talk to him." Derek wiped his hands with a napkin. "If he's not involved in the murders, then he needs to come forward."

"What about the link between these murders and my assault?" Piper asked. She clasped her hands together in her lap and the knuckles turned white. "Was the killer telling the truth? Was he responsible for attacking me?"

"I don't think so." Emilia shot Piper a sympathetic look. Not so long ago, Emilia was hunted by a serial killer bent on terrorizing her. Bennett had saved her, and now the two were happily married. "I've thoroughly reviewed the case file from your assault. Derek, excuse me, Sheriff Martinez—"

"Nope. It's Derek."

Emilia smiled and then nodded before continuing, "Derek did an excellent job. There were bloody fingerprints left behind at the scene. The blood was yours, Piper, but the fingerprints matched Lionel Islip. I had the lab run them again, just to be certain. They came back a match." She removed a report from the file folder and handed it to Piper to review. "Elena and Gerdie's killer is not the same man who assaulted you. However, and this is where I need to be cautious, it's possible Lionel had a partner."

Piper's brow creased in confusion. "But there was only one attacker."

"The other could have been waiting outside, acting as a guard. It would explain how he knew the specific details of your assault. Details that weren't included in the police report."

"There's some evidence to support the theory of a partner," Derek added, scraping a hand over his chin. "An elderly man spotted two men running down the back side of the neighborhood around the time of your assault. I followed up with him, but he couldn't provide any more information. His vision was poor, and he didn't get a look at their faces. None of the other neighbors could confirm the sighting. Since you were certain there was only one assailant, I disregarded it." He shook his head. "I'm sorry. I screwed up."

"Doesn't sound that way to me." Piper's tone was gentle and understanding. "I would've done the same, given the same set of facts. Hindsight is always twenty-twenty, and no investigation is perfect."

"Agreed." Lieutenant Rodriguez ran a hand over her ponytail before tossing the dark strands over her shoul-der. "Wally is our main suspect, but there are others to pursue. Todd is one. But we could be completely off base and there's a third person responsible who isn't on our radar yet. Based on the phone call to Piper yesterday, the killer wants to keep us chasing our tails. Has anyone questioned Marcus Reed? If we're right, and someone encouraged him to shoot Piper, then maybe he can tell us who it was."

"I tried but didn't get anywhere." Derek blew out a breath. "Marcus was pretty out of it at the time. The drugs had worn off, but he wasn't mentally stable yet. He's still in the hospital. I can swing by there today and give it another go."

"No, I'll do it," Piper said. "Marcus and I have known each other since I was a kid. I used to give him food when I lived with my mom and we had some to spare. He may be more upfront with me."

"I'll go with you." Jackson wasn't letting her out of his sight.

Lieutenant Rodriguez nodded. "Good. Now for the rest of you, let's assign tasks. Emilia, are you working on a profile of the killer?"

"I am." Emilia's gaze swept the room. "But there's something you all should know. This case is urgent. Whoever is responsible for these murders won't stop. Moreover, his fixation on Piper isn't imagined."

Jackson's gut clenched. He leaned forward. "Emilia, do you think this guy has killed before? Before Elena, I mean?"

She nodded. "I'd be surprised if he hasn't. Piper's assault was the beginning. Since then he's been practicing. Now he's an expert. Elena and Gerdie's murders were well-executed and well-planned. He knows what he's doing." She held his gaze. "Be careful. Both of you. He wants Piper, but won't hesitate to kill anyone standing in his path."

His mind whirled, thinking back on the attacks, including the bombing. Something that he'd been questioning suddenly made sense. "He waited until Piper was clear of Elena's house before igniting the bomb."

Piper inhaled. Her gaze shot to him. "What?"

Emilia nodded. "That's what I think too. You were the target that day, Jackson. He wants you away from Piper, and he's willing to kill you to do it."

TWENTY

The hospital was a bustle of activity. Piper shook off her umbrella before entering through the sliding doors. Plastic bags hung from a rack and she grabbed one, handing it to Jackson for his umbrella, before slipping one over her own. The scent of bleach and antiseptic seemed to permeate the air. White-tile floors shone in the florescent lighting. Goosebumps pebbled on Piper's arms. She wasn't fond of hospitals.

Jackson fell into step beside her as they navigated passed the busy emergency room to the elevators. Marcus had officially been arrested for attempted murder, and until a judge decided his fate at a bail hearing, was under armed guard in his hospital room.

Piper hit the button for the fifth floor, and the cabin rose. She glanced out of the corner of her eye at Jackson. He'd been quiet on the car ride over, his expression wedged in a permanent scowl. Piper elbowed him. "You're doing that thing again."

"What thing?"

Her mouth quirked. "Brooding."

"Considering I was told half an hour ago there's a killer hunting you down, is it really so surprising?" Jackson hooked his thumbs in his pockets and rocked back on his heels. "If it was up to me, I'd lock you in the house behind a set of armed Texas Rangers until this whole thing was done. Do you know how many of my colleagues have been in this kind of situation? Almost all of them."

She blinked. "What do you mean?"

"Most of company A is married or engaged. They met their significant other under dangerous circumstances. Fell in love while protecting a woman in danger." He turned to face her and cupped her cheek with his warm palm. "And every one of those women nearly died. Do you understand the odds aren't with us, Piper? Sometime, someone in Company A is going to be on the losing end of this equation." His gaze searched her face before he leaned forward to touch her forehead with his. "I don't want it to be me. I don't want to lose you."

Her knees weakened at the tenderness in his tone. She wanted to fling herself in his arms and never let go. "I can't, Jackson. I ran away once, and as a result, more women died. If I'd been here…"

He pulled back. "This isn't your fault. Just like it's not Derek's."

"Maybe not, but it doesn't change how I feel. Elena died in my arms. If our theory is right, maybe the killer purposefully picked that day, that location, because he knew I ran in the nature preserve."

Piper had been mulling that over since the task force meeting. She couldn't prove it, but the idea felt right. She'd been targeted right from the beginning. The killer was playing a game with her, and she had every intention of finishing it.

"Elena and Gerdie deserve justice. I want to get it for them." She also needed to prove she was stronger than the killer. Piper couldn't put it into words, but the assault ten years ago had left a shadow over her life. "I promise to be careful and to use my training. The last thing I want is for someone else—like you—to be caught in the crossfire."

The idea of Jackson hurt or killed was terrifying. Piper was falling in love with him. Or, if she was being honest, maybe she never stopped loving him. It was an impossible dilemma—their relationship couldn't last—but her heart wouldn't listen to reason or logic.

The elevator dinged, and the doors swished open. Jackson stepped off first, holding out a hand to show she should wait. His gaze swept the area and then he waved her forward. "What room is Marcus in?"

"510." She pointed to a sign. "It's around the corner."

A deputy was stationed outside the door. Mike O'Neal. Piper greeted him and introduced Jackson. "We need to question Marcus. How is he?"

"Much better. Today he seems with it." Mike adjusted his duty belt, and the leather creaked. "He's got one hand cuffed to the bed, but I would use caution. He was violent with the nurses and the doctors when he was brought in. They had to sedate him initially."

"Understood. Thanks." Piper knocked on the door and then entered the room.

Marcus was sitting up in bed watching a sitcom. His hair was pushed away from his face, but he sported a new beard along his chin. The hospital gown swallowed his thin frame and one skinny leg peeked out from under the covers. A heart machine beeped regularly while an IV delivered fluids into his right arm. His eyes widened at the sight of Piper. He jerked upright. The handcuff securing him to the bed frame rattled.

"I'm glad you're here, Piper. I'm so sorry for what happened. I didn't know what I was doing." His expression was beseeching. "You have to believe me. I've never fired a gun in my life. It all feels like a dream."

"Hold on, Marcus, there are some things we have to take care of." Piper pulled out her cell phone and activated the recording app. She announced herself and everyone in the room before reading the Miranda warning. Since Marcus was under arrest and in custody, he needed to be advised of his rights before any questioning could take place. Once that was done, Piper asked, "Do you agree to wave your rights, Marcus?"

"Yes. I want to help you figure out what happened."

"According to the doctor, you were high on methamphetamine."

She kept her distance, standing at the foot of the bed, well out of striking range. Jackson lingered near the door like a silent sentry. Piper appreciated that he hung back and let her take the lead.

Marcus looked down, twisting a bedsheet in-between his fingers. "I don't remember taking anything."

"What do you remember?"

"I was hanging out with Wally Hutchinson in his brother's house. Next thing I know, I woke up here. I don't even know how I got to the police station or where I got the gun."

Piper's heart skipped a beat. Marcus's confession confirmed at least one of the Hutchinson brothers was involved. "What about Todd? Was he there?"

Marcus shook his head. "No. I remember thinking it was weird that we were hanging out at Todd's house without him there, but Wally crashes there from time to time."

"Did Wally give you the meth, Marcus?"

Before he could answer, the hospital room door swung open and Paul Kingston strolled in. His cologne was heavy and matched the dark scowl etched on his face. "What are you doing questioning my client without my permission, detective?"

"You represent Marcus?" Jackson stepped forward, his tone incredulous. "Since when?"

"Since I was appointed this morning by the judge at the bail hearing. My firm often represents clients pro bono as part of our community service. I've been Mr. Reed's attorney before, so the judge thought it made sense to appoint me in this matter as well." He waved Mike forward. "My client has been released on bail, which has already been posted with a bondsman by his aunt. Please remove these handcuffs immediately. And all questioning will stop."

Marcus sat up straighter. "But I want to help Piper—"

Paul placed a hand on his shoulder. "No. First we'll talk and if there's something important to pass on to law enforcement, then we'll discuss the best way to handle it."

"You don't have to listen to him, Marcus." Piper kept her eyes on the older man in the bed. She'd given him food, been kind to him. They had a connection that clearly mattered to Marcus. "You can decide to answer my questions anyway—"

"Do not speak to my client." Paul whirled on her. His scathing look sent a shiver down her spine. "This interview is over, Detective Jensen. Get out. Now." He got between Piper and Marcus, blocking the criminal's view of her. "Trust me, Mr. Reed. I've never steered you wrong before and I won't now."

To Piper's dismay, Marcus nodded and leaned back against the bed. "I'll do as my attorney says."

She hit the stop button on her cell to end the recording. "Get well, Marcus, and if you decide you want to speak to me, then call the sheriff's department."

"Goodbye, Detective Jensen." Paul moved toward her, waving her back with his hands. "You too, Ranger Barker. Get out of this room."

The moment they went into the hall, Paul slammed the hospital door shut.

Piper breathed out. "Well that didn't go as planned,

but we got some useful information out of Marcus. Do you think his statement is enough to convince a judge to give us a search warrant for Todd's house?"

"I do." Jackson tossed his keys toward her while simultaneously pulling his cell phone out of his pocket. "You drive. I'll prepare the warrant."

Fifteen minutes later, Piper pulled up to Todd's house. The place looked abandoned and sadder in the rain. Wind blew a few of the beer cans against the chain link fence. Todd's dog was missing. It also hadn't been seen since the bombing. He'd probably taken the animal with him. Piper prayed the poor thing was okay. The Hutchinsons abused women. She couldn't imagine what they might do to a helpless animal.

Jackson was on hold with the judge, who was reviewing the warrant. His fingers tapped against the dash in a nervous dance. Piper had already called Derek and informed him of what they'd discovered by questioning Marcus. Several Texas Rangers were en route to help aid with the search once the warrant went through.

Her gaze drifted to Elena's house. It was a pile of blackened rubble.

Everything started with her murder. Elena's. Or was Piper's assault the catalyst? Ten years had gone by. Why did the killer wait all this time to strike again? Had he chosen Elena simply because she was blonde and blue-eyed? Or was she more integral to the puzzle than the killer wanted them to believe?

"Thank you, judge. Have a nice afternoon." Jackson hung up with a big smile on his face. "Warrant came through. Let's wait for backup, and then we'll start the search."

"There's backup now." Piper pointed as several official state vehicles turned the corner.

Rain pelted her cowboy hat as she and Jackson strolled up the main walkway to Todd's house, followed by several deputies from her department. Bennett and Luke circled around back with their own set of deputies. Everyone had their gun drawn. Todd was considered armed and dangerous.

Jackson pounded on the door. "Police! We have a search warrant for the premises!"

A few more knocks yielded no reply. Jackson stepped back, and one of the deputies used a battering ram to break down the door. It flew inward. Like they'd been working together forever, Piper and Jackson entered the house. She took left; he took right.

It was surprisingly neat and tidy inside. The beam of Piper's light washed over a couch and a cracked leather recliner. A brand-new widescreen TV and a gaming station rested next to a fireplace. It smelled like stale beer and old trash. The back door crashed open, followed by Bennett and Luke entering the kitchen.

"Sheriff's Department!" Piper shouted down the hallway leading to the back of the house. "We have a search warrant. If you're on the premises, make yourself known."

No response. Jackson led the way to the first closed door. He grabbed the handle and twisted quickly, sweeping low as he entered. Piper followed, sweeping high. Her pulse skipped several beats as the beam of her flashlight washed over a long table along the back wall. It was covered in wires and electronics.

"Clear!" Jackson shouted.

Echoes of the same rang out as every room was checked. Todd wasn't there.

Piper lowered her handgun and stepped closer to the table. She studied the equipment. "He was building bombs." She glanced at Jackson, her mind racing. "What if we're focusing on the wrong brother? Todd went to high school with us, along with Lionel Islip. They likely knew each other. Plus, Todd was at home when the explosion at Elena's happened."

"It's possible. Marcus never told us Wally gave him the gun. He only remembers being here with Wally. Todd could've returned while he was high." Jackson blew out a breath. "Then again, Marcus also said Wally crashes here from time to time. Who's to say he doesn't use Todd's place to build his bombs? A lot easier to do it here than in the pay-by-the-week motel he was staying in."

She nodded. "True."

"I never liked Todd though. Especially the way he looked at you." Jackson stepped toward her and a click echoed through the room.

He froze. Fear tightened his features.

Piper instinctively moved toward him.

"No!" Jackson's tone was sharp, but he didn't move a centimeter. Sweat beaded on his brow. "Don't come any closer. You and the rest of the team need to evacuate the house immediately. And call the bomb squad."

Her breath hitched as she tried to make sense of what he was telling her. Fear ordered her back, but love demanded she move closer. As a result, she was frozen in place. Her mind wouldn't accept what her body already knew.

Jackson met her gaze. "Get out, Piper. Now. I'm standing on a pressure plate. If I move, or even so much as breathe wrong, this entire house is going to explode."

Sweat trickled down Jackson's back.

Every muscle in his body was locked. It'd been twenty minutes since he'd stepped on the pressure plate and there was no end to this living nightmare in sight. The bomb squad was en route, but meantime, he was left alone with nothing but his thoughts. The stench of his fear mingled with the scent of trash. Rain beat against the window. A cockroach, emboldened by his lack of movement, scurried closer. Jackson watched it with trepidation. If that thing crawled up his pant leg...

Don't think about it.

He squeezed his eyes shut. "God, thank you for giving everyone a chance to get out of the house safely. If this is how I die, then I accept Your will—"

"This is absolutely *not* how you're going to die."

Jackson's eyes snapped open. Derek entered the room, wearing a bomb suit. The thick padding added bulk to his already thick frame, and coupled with the helmet and shield, made him look like some kind of alien. A walkie-talkie in his hand crackled. Derek pressed the button on the side. "Jackson is holding still. What's the ETA?"

"Unable to determine, sheriff. We're working on gaining access to the bomb located under the house."

"Move quickly, but not so fast you blow us to heaven, got it?"

A chuckle came over the line. "Yes, sir."

Jackson blinked as sweat dripped into his eyes. The temperature in the house was sweltering. His mouth was cotton dry and his muscles trembled. "You need to get out of here, Derek. Procedure requires you to stand clear until the bomb squad—"

"Don't bother lecturing me. I already got it from the head of the bomb squad." He set his flashlight down on the table. "Want to know the best part of being sheriff? I'm in charge of this jurisdiction. No one outranks me. I'm here, Jackson, and I'm staying until we walk out of this house together."

Jackson clenched his jaw to keep the tears burning his eyes in check. "My dad was right about you. He always said you'd make the best sheriff Rock Fort has ever seen."

Derek chuckled. "Your dad cussed me out more than once for putting you in danger during our ride-alongs. Remember that time I had to chase down the robber and he doubled-back? You tackled him."

Jackson smiled at the memory. He'd been eighteen, fresh out of high school, and had gotten special permission to ride along with Derek to learn what it was like to be in law enforcement. "You nearly kicked my behind for getting out of the car."

"I told you to stay inside."

"But he was running right past me!" Jackson's heart skipped a beat as his muscles nearly loosened. "Don't crack jokes. I can't laugh." He fell silent. "My dad would really curse you out if he knew what was happening right now."

"I know. That's why I'm in here. If you die, I die too, and that way I won't have to face your dad's wrath."

Jackson smothered another laugh to keep his muscles from moving. "Stop, Derek. Please."

"You started it." Derek fell silent for a moment. Then his mouth quirked. "So you and Piper, huh?"

Jackson groaned. "Another topic I can't get into."

"Yeah, the Jensen women are a tough breed. Always have been. My theory is you just keep pushing until they finally let you in. It takes time, mind you." His gaze turned distant. "Years in my case. But I'm hoping one day Ava will finally realize the man she was looking for was standing right in front of her the whole time."

"Have you tried telling her how you feel?"

Derek's brows arched. "How's that plan working for you?"

"Good point."

Piper was still running scared. Jackson didn't know how to topple her walls. He respected Derek's dedication, but sticking around for years didn't seem like a good answer to the problem. There had to be another way. If he survived this incident, he intended to figure it out.

He was in love with Piper. It'd taken standing on a pressure plate with a bomb attached to make things crystal clear. He'd lived his life without her—could do it again if he had to—but it's not what he wanted. He wanted a life with her. Marriage. Kids. The whole fairy tale.

Of course, telling her that was a surefire way to send Piper into a panic.

"I checked on Piper. For years after she left town, I called Grandma Mary for updates. I was hurt by her actions, but I always cared. Sometimes I wonder if I'm a glutton for punishment." Jackson blinked more sweat away from his eyes. "My mom abandoned me when I was a kid. Now I'm chasing after a woman determined not to be caught. I'm sure a therapist would have a field day with that."

Derek grunted. "I'm no therapist, and I can't speak about your mother or her actions, but I know Piper cares deeply about you. She tried to get back into this house after clearing everyone out. Bennett had to physically restrain her, and the only reason she's not in here instead of me is because I threatened to arrest her."

Jackson's gut clenched. Deep inside, part of him had wondered if the feelings between them were one-sided, or at the very least, Jackson cared more than Piper. Clearly that wasn't true. The brave woman tried to run back into a house with a bomb inside it. To be with him.

"She's not pushing you away because she's difficult,"

Derek continued. "She does it because she's scared. Ava and Piper never had any love or security before they moved in with Grandma Mary. The abuse they suffered before children's services removed them from their mother's home... it would turn your hair white. I've read all the reports. Both of them have holes in the memories. A trauma response."

"Why did they bounce between Grandma Mary's and their mother's if the abuse was so awful?"

"Because the system is screwed up. Their mom would get her act together just enough to have them returned. Within a month or two, they'd be back with Mary. It was a constant merry-go-round. And the worst part? They really loved their mom. I mean, Piper was there, at the house, delivering groceries when she was attacked. She has a heart of gold, but every time she turned around, bam." Derek slapped his hands together. "She'd get knocked down."

Jackson took in every word. He'd never considered how devastating it must've been for Piper to be constantly shifted between her mother and Grandma Mary's house. There was no security. No safety. Nothing steady or dependable. The minute she got comfortable, she'd been torn away from Grandma Mary and shipped back to her mother's. Through it all, she studied and worked hard to get into college.

Then the attack happened. Jackson knew it'd devastated Piper, but he'd never understood the full picture. She fought and crawled and battled to get her life under control, only to have it all ripped away again.

Did she think it would always be like that? Every time her life was stable, something would tear it apart again?

His heart broke. No wonder Piper was so terrified of their relationship.

The radio crackled, and a voice mumbled something Jackson couldn't make out. Derek lifted the device and pressed the button. "Sheriff here. Go ahead."

"We've gained access to the underside of the house and are determining the best course of action to disable the bomb. We'll contact you once we have a plan."

"The faster, the better, gentlemen. It's hot in here and the cockroaches are getting aggressive." Derek shooed one away from Jackson.

"Understood."

Jackson's muscles trembled, and an ache had started in his leg, indicating a cramp was not far off. He didn't know how long he could continue standing motionless. It'd been almost an hour, and his body was at an awkward angle with his balance pitched more on his right foot than his left. His shirt was soaked with sweat.

God, give me strength.

If he triggered the bomb, it would kill Derek along with the techs underneath the house. Jackson had to hold it together. For them. For himself. And for Piper.

He couldn't die without telling her he loved her. Piper might panic, but at least she would know the truth.

After that... Jackson had no clue. He couldn't think that far ahead.

The future—like everything else—was in God's hands.

TWENTY-TWO

Piper had never prayed so hard in her entire life. She'd begged and pleaded. It wasn't right, but she'd also bargained with God. Anything to move from one breath to the next without completely having a breakdown. It was torture, standing close enough to see the house, but being unable to do anything to help Jackson.

At any moment, he could die.

And he would never know how much he meant to her.

Tears welled in her eyes. She'd pushed Jackson away, hoping that these feelings between them would eventually wither and die. Instead, they'd only grown. He'd wriggled past all her defenses somehow. Not even ten years of separation—and her own stupid decision to bail on their relationship—could ruin it. Piper was terrified of what a future with Jackson looked like. Her own short-comings would surely screw everything up, but in this moment, she couldn't care about any of that. All that mattered was that Jackson would die without ever knowing she loved him.

God, I'm so lost. I've tried to be strong. I picked myself back up over and over again, but if Jackson dies, I fear this may break me for good.

A dozen feet away, Jackson's colleagues were in a prayer circle. Bennett didn't join the group. He stayed by Piper's side like a sentry. To prevent her from entering the house? Or protect her from a potential attack from the killer? She wasn't sure, but his steady and constant presence allowed her to focus on her prayers. Deputies and other state police kept control of the scene while the bomb squad conferred in small groups. Several men in thick suits and face masks headed for the house. Rain pelted Piper's head. She barely felt it.

"Piper!"

She turned. Ava hurried toward her on limping steps. Her face was red and puffy from crying. Weston walked beside her, holding an umbrella, worry etched on every inch of his features. Piper moved to intercept them. "What are you doing here?"

"Ava insisted on coming," Weston explained. "We saw what was happening on the news. Mary is with the kids, and Cole is keeping them safe."

"Is he in there?" Ava gripped Piper's arms with enough force to leave bruises. Panic swelled in her voice. "Is Derek inside the house?"

She nodded and fresh tears filled her eyes, shocking Piper to the core. Ava almost never cried. She gathered her sister in a hug. "It's going to be okay."

"Don't you dare lie to me, Piper." She shook off the embrace. "What kind of man goes inside a house knowing there's a bomb? That's a new level of stupidity right there. I knew this kind of thing would happen. I told myself not to get emotionally involved, not to develop feelings beyond friendship. He has a dangerous job. I have to protect myself. But look at me!" She waved a hand over her tear-stained face. "I fell in love with him and now I'm a wreck because he's about to be blown up!"

Piper's heart broke for her sister. She'd suspected Ava had feelings for Derek, but she didn't realize how deep they ran. No wonder her sister was in a panic. "Derek went back inside to help Jackson. He didn't want him to be alone."

Her sister cried harder. "He's brave and stupid."

Piper hugged her sister again. "What would Grandma Mary tell us to do in this situation?"

"To hold on to our faith." Ava sniffed and then pulled back, her eyes widening. "Oh, Piper, I'm sorry. Jackson's inside too. I was so caught up—"

"It's okay. I've been so worried about Jackson, I didn't even think to call you about Derek. I'm sorry you had to find out from the news."

"There's movement," Bennett announced. Rain gathered on the brim of his hat and ran down the back onto his jacket. His focus was on the house. Bomb squad techs high-fived each other.

Piper's gaze shot to the front door. No one was there, but she started running. Past the crime scene tape marking off the blast zone and through the gate on the side of Todd's yard. Someone yelled at her. She ignored them. Beer cans scattered as they were kicked away by the force of her steps.

Jackson appeared in the doorway. Whole. Unharmed.

A cheer went up from the watching crowd, along with thunderous applause, but Piper barely heard it. Like a laser beam, she focused on the gorgeous man stepping off of the porch and into the rain. He saw her coming and opened his arms wide, catching her mid step and swinging her around before lowering her feet back to the ground.

She kissed him. The worry and fear melted into passion and need. Every emotion she couldn't put into words went into that kiss. Ten years of longing and love. Time slowed down until nothing existed beyond the two of them. Her heart soared as Jackson deepened the kiss, drawing her close, not letting her go until they were both breathless.

He pulled back just enough to stare into her eyes. "I love you, Piper."

Her heart stuttered and then took off like a bird in flight. "I love you too." Tears swelled in her eyes as she kissed him again. "I have no idea where we go from here, but I can't care about that right now. I love you and have for ten years. I think I'll love you for the rest of my life."

He trembled as if she'd shocked him, and then a broad smile brightened his entire face. "The rest of your life, huh? I can work with that."

Before she could even think of a response, he bent his

head and captured her lips again. There was no room for fear or worry when she was in his arms.

There was only love.

———

Hours later, Piper sipped coffee in the bullpen of the sheriff's department. Her gaze was locked on Derek's office. The blinds were closed, as was the door. All around her was controlled chaos. Deputies and other state personnel were filing reports and discussing the case.

"What are you doing?" Jackson strolled up, a smile playing on his lips. He'd changed clothes, and the green button-down highlighted the stunning color of his eyes.

Piper grinned back, twisting in her chair. "Spying on my sister. Ava and Derek went into his office twenty minutes ago and are still talking."

Apparently, Piper and Jackson weren't the only couple to share a passionate kiss after the bomb was disarmed. Derek, unfortunately, was then tasked with handling the media fallout, as well as taking charge of the scene. He and Ava hadn't had a chance to discuss everything until now.

Neither had Piper and Jackson. She'd buried herself in paperwork and reviewing the updated reports from other members of the task force. There were hundreds of witness interviews and thousands of leads to follow up on. It felt insurmountable.

"Have you seen what Emilia discovered?" Piper set

her mug down and shifted through the paperwork to find the profiler's report. "She also located two murders in the surrounding counties. The victims were female, blonde, and blue-eyed. Both were beaten and shot. The bodies were dumped in a wooded area and found years later."

Jackson leaned against her desk. "So we're dealing with a serial killer."

"Definitely seems that way. My assault was ten years ago. These two murders happened after that, one five years later, one seven years later. Both women disappeared from a bar."

"Like Gerdie."

She nodded. "Grady followed up with the bartender at the Watering Hole, which is where Wally and Todd went on the afternoon Elena was murdered. He confirmed Wally was the one talking with Gerdie." She twisted back and forth in her chair. "Wally's former roommate—the one he had during his time in the military —also confirmed Wally learned how to build bombs from him. He must be the killer."

"Not necessarily. The two brothers could be working together."

"Todd's an alcoholic. Does he have the brains and wherewithal to plan several murders?"

"Alcoholics can build up a tolerance. You'd be surprised how functional they can be." Jackson frowned. "I don't think we should ignore the possibility that Todd is behind all of this. Either way, I bet they're hiding out together. We find one brother, we'll find the other."

Piper nodded in agreement. "So far, they've avoided

detection. I can't imagine where they're hiding out. In some kind of cave?"

Jackson's phone rang. His brows creased when he glanced at the screen. "It's Shawn."

He answered the call. Piper couldn't hear what Shawn was saying, but judging from the look of surprise on Jackson's face, it was unexpected. He tried to get Shawn to tell him something over the phone, but the man obviously refused.

She anxiously waited for Jackson to hang up and then said, "What happened?"

"He wants to meet in private at the nature preserve parking lot on the west side. Shawn claims to have information that will help the case."

"Do you believe him?" Piper didn't trust the Kingstons any farther than she could throw them. "After the way Paul acted in Marcus's hospital room, I'm not convinced the Kingstons aren't covering something up. It's possible a serial killer targeted Elena randomly, but it certainly comes at a convenient time for Shawn. This could be a trap. You can't go to that meeting alone."

Jackson's mouth quirked up. "I wasn't planning on it."

TWENTY-THREE

Jackson's windshield wipers swished rhythmically. It was just after dusk, but the constant rain made the darkness press closer. The parking lot was empty. He'd rolled his window down just a smidge, and the scent of pine scented with rain swept in on the breeze. Shawn was late.

Piper sighed. "Do you think he changed his mind?"

Jackson shrugged. "We'll give him a few minutes. This is a clandestine meeting. Maybe he had some trouble slipping away unnoticed." He picked up his cell phone and pressed a button on the screen to activate the walkie-talkie app connecting him to his teammates hiding in the woods. "Any sign of a vehicle?"

"Negative." Bennett growled. "Wish this rain would stop. I've spent half the day in the mud."

"Well, it won't end anytime soon," Daniel interjected. "There's another thunderstorm heading our way. It's going to get worse before it gets better."

Jackson grimaced. High winds and heavy downpours

could be dangerous, especially for his teammates out in the woods who were exposed to the elements. "What's the ETA on that storm?"

"Half an hour. We've got time, just not much of it."

"Copy. We'll give Shawn another five minutes. If he doesn't show up by then, we'll arrange for another meeting in a more controlled location." Jackson hated to pull the plug, but he wouldn't put his colleagues through unnecessary risk. Facing off with a potential killer in a deserted parking lot was bad enough. Doing it during a thunderstorm was a step too far. "Signal if you see movement."

He clicked off the talk button on the app and set his phone back down in the cup holder. Piper cleared her throat and adjusted her weight on the seat. She was nervous, and Jackson suspected not all of her anxiety was about Shawn. He took her hand. "Now you're doing it."

"What?"

"Brooding."

She laughed, the sound light and musical. Jackson realized how little she laughed. Piper was always so serious, as if the weight of the world rested on her shoulders. He wanted to help carry her burdens, whatever they were. Jackson threaded his fingers through hers and rubbed his thumb over the back of her hand. "It might help if you talk about it. We've got time."

She glanced down at their joined hands and then met his gaze. "It's about you and me."

"I figured."

"I love you, Jackson. I know that with certainty, but

everything else... how this will work... I don't have a clue. You deserve so much better than me. I'm riddled with problems, and they'll only drag you down." He opened his mouth to answer her, but she cut him off with a shake of her head. "Wait, let me say this. Nothing about my life is normal. My feelings get lodged inside, and I don't know how to let them out. It's not easy for me to trust. I know there are good marriages, but I have no idea how to build one. My first instinct is to protect you because I know it's only a matter of time before I screw everything up."

He gently squeezed her hand. "Is that why you left ten years ago?"

"Of course. My PTSD was out of control. No one could touch me and I was jumping at every shadow. It made everything worse." She bit her lip. "Like I said, you deserve better than me."

Jackson's first instinct was to argue. There was no one better than Piper. The loyalty she had for her family, the dedication to her job, the gentleness she used with her niece and nephew... she was by far the best woman he'd ever known. But he sensed none of that would convince her, so he took a different tack instead. "Don't you think that's my decision?"

She blinked, obviously caught off-guard. "What?"

"I've decided you're the woman for me, Piper, and there's nothing you can do about it. Whether I love you or not is my choice. So, the way I see it, you and I can figure out a way to make this work, or you can cut me off again. Run away from this. From us. I'm praying you won't though. Because I don't want to live my life without you."

Jackson turned to face her. "And for the record, I don't deserve better than you. I'm messed up too. We all have our scars and our wounds. My mom ran out on me when I was eight. She left me behind like a discarded shoe. There are times I doubt myself and my worth. When your mom doesn't love you…"

How could he explain the depth of that wound? There were no words for it.

Piper sighed and gently squeezed his hand. "Yeah, I know."

She did know. Jackson breathed out. "I also don't know what it takes to make a marriage work. All I know is that I love you. I believe in us."

His cell phone chirped. Jackson was irritated by the interruption, but there was nothing to be done about it. He retrieved the device from the cup holder and hit the button.

"We've got movement," Daniel said in a low voice. "Mercedes heading to the parking lot."

Shawn drove a Mercedes. Jackson's muscles tensed and he glanced at Piper. "It's go time."

She unbuckled her seat belt and twisted between the seats, landing in a heap on the back bench. Dropping to the floor, she pulled her handgun. A safety precaution in case Shawn tried to hurt Jackson.

Headlights turned into the parking lot. Jackson's heart rate quickened. "Going dark." He lowered the volume on his phone but left the connection to his teammates open. Daniel and Bennett would hear everything. Jackson also quickly opened a recording app on his phone before clicking the screen off. Texas was a one-party consent state. Shawn didn't have to know he was being recorded.

Layer after layer of security. He prayed it wouldn't be necessary.

The Mercedes pulled up next to Jackson's vehicle. Shawn hopped out and quickly jumped into the passenger seat. He swiped water off his face. "Thanks for meeting me."

Jackson purposefully didn't look at Piper. He didn't want Shawn to realize she was there. Instead, he focused on his childhood friend. The lighting was dim, but even in the darkness, it was obvious Shawn was exhausted. His hair was mussed and his tie askew. Dark circles shadowed the area under his eyes. He nervously scanned the parking lot as if the boogie man was about to jump out of the woods.

Was someone out there? Was Shawn working with Wally? Or Todd?

If so, hopefully Daniel or Bennett would spot the man before he could carry out a plan of attack. Jackson forced himself to focus on the matter at hand. "What's going on, Shawn? What information do you have that you couldn't give me over the phone?"

"I need some questions answered first. Is Wally responsible for Elena's death?"

"He's a suspect." Jackson didn't mention Todd was also a suspect. He didn't owe Shawn any explanations, nor was he going to let his friend ask all the questions. "Did your wife really know about the affair?"

He was quiet for a long moment. "No. My father convinced her to lie by making her a partner in our law firm." Shawn sighed. "My marriage has been on the rocks for a long time. Melanie broke her vows first, and I was so mad that I did the same with Elena. It wasn't right. I know that now. But I was too caught up in everything to understand how much damage I was doing." He rubbed his eyes, and a sob rose in his throat. "I loved her, you know. Elena. I wanted to divorce my wife and marry her."

"Why didn't you?"

"Because of my father." He swiped at his wet cheeks as anger filled his tone. "He would've cut me off financially for marrying Elena. She's below us, according to him. I'd lose the firm. I did my best to explain that to Elena, but she..." Shawn sighed. "She wanted more. I couldn't give it to her."

"That didn't stop you from calling and texting her dozens of times."

He shrugged. "I wanted her back. Do you have any idea what it's like to walk into work, see the woman you were meant to be with, and not be able to do anything about it? I was losing my mind. It was the first time I was truly in love with someone. It was also the first time I'd ever had my heart broken."

Jackson could believe that. Shawn had always treated his girlfriends as interchangeable. "You don't love your wife?"

"At one point, maybe I did. But things quickly soured after we got married. I realized..." He blew out a breath.

"I married her because my father wanted it. Because it was expected. Melanie is from a good family with wealth and ties to the governor. The marriage made sense on paper. It was a disaster in real life."

Everything he said made sense, but Jackson had the lingering impression, once again, that he was being handled. Shawn was Paul's son after all. He learned to manipulate a situation to his advantage from the best. "What do you want from me, Shawn?"

"I want to know that you're going to do everything possible to get justice for Elena. I want her killer caught."

"We didn't have to meet in a deserted parking lot for me to tell you that."

"What evidence do you have that proves Wally is Elena's killer?"

His gaze narrowed. "Are you seriously going to tell me you don't know what's going on with the investigation? I know you have contacts in the sheriff's department that are feeding you information."

"I need to hear it from you."

"I can't tell you that, Shawn." Jackson was growing tired of the subterfuge. "This is an ongoing investigation and you're a civilian. Two women are dead. If you have information that can help, then give it to me and let's stop wasting time."

Shawn's leg jittered. The silence stretched out. Jackson let it.

Finally, Shawn sighed. "If you ever tell anyone this information came from me, I'll deny it." He reached into his pocket and pulled out a slip of paper. "There's a cabin the Hutchinson brothers use from time to time. I learned about it during Wally's last domestic violence case. The cabin and its location is covered under attorney-client privilege." He met Jackson's gaze. "I'm breaking dozens of ethical rules and putting my law license on the line by giving you this information, but I can't let Elena's murderer go free."

He slapped the paper down on the console. "You'll find the brothers hiding out there."

Before Jackson could say a word, Shawn opened the car door and hopped out. He ran to his Mercedes and got in. Tires squealed as he pulled out of the parking lot. His taillights flashed and then disappeared into the night.

Piper popped her head up as Jackson turned on his overhead light. An address was scrawled on the paper. Jackson studied it before glancing up at the road. His stomach swirled with anxiety. It was too good to be true.

"A trap?" Piper asked, echoing his own suspicions.

"I don't know."

TWENTY-FOUR

Jackson pulled his SUV to the side of the road behind a large armored vehicle filled with SWAT. Aerial satellite images of the area had been combed over by the team. There was nothing between this road and the cabin. He killed the engine. The sound of crickets and forest nightlife resumed. It was four in the morning, and he should be exhausted, but adrenaline kept the tiredness away.

Daniel hopped out of the passenger side. Felicity, Grady, and Bennett poured from the back seats. Jackson popped the rear hatch so they could access the bullet-proof vests and equipment that'd been loaded in preparation for the raid, but he didn't get out of the vehicle himself. Instead, he called Piper.

She answered on the first ring. "I'm still mad I can't be there."

His lips curved into a smile. "It's better you're there to keep your family safe. Don't tell him I said this, but

Cole's aim isn't that great yet. He needs to spend more time in the shooting range."

Weston's wife, Avery, had an unexpected medical complication. She would be fine, but he had to return home to help care for her and his newborn daughter. Cole was more than capable of keeping Ava and the kids safe, but Jackson felt better knowing Piper was there too. He worried the team was walking into a trap. It was also possible this excursion, an hour away from Rock Fort, was a distraction designed to draw resources away, so Piper and her family were vulnerable to an attack.

Jackson had debated leaving her, but it was Piper who'd encouraged him to go. If Shawn's information was correct, the threat against her could be eliminated within the hour.

"Be safe, Jackson. I love you."

Those words never failed to make his heart skip a beat. "I love you too."

He hung up. Guilt and indecision warred within him. Had he made a mistake leaving her behind? Jackson gave himself a mental shake. That was just irrational fear talking. Piper was at home, behind locked doors and an armed security system, with a Texas Ranger guarding her. She was safe.

He exited the vehicle. The thunderstorm had lightened to a drizzle. Grady handed him a bulletproof vest. "Piper okay?"

"She's mad about being left behind, but otherwise, she's fine." Jackson slipped the vest on and secured it. "Have you spoken with Tara?"

"She's praying for us as we speak." Grady slapped him on the shoulder before grabbing a rifle. Jackson followed suit, and they joined the rest of the law enforcement officers.

Derek, also dressed in tactical gear, stood at the front. "The cabin is five miles to the north. We'll split up as per the plan, surround the cabin, and then approach by foot. Each team takes a bomb detection dog with you. The perpetrators are considered armed and dangerous. Everyone use caution. Any questions?"

No one spoke.

Derek nodded. "Be safe and godspeed."

Nerves jumping, Jackson and the rest of his team divided up by predesignated units. Then they all loaded into the back of several armored vehicles and drove roughly four miles to the cabin. At some point, the other vehicles split off. Everyone was approaching from different angles. The bomb detection dog assigned to them, Lisa, was a beautiful German shepherd. She led the way into the forest.

Jackson's boots sank into the muddy ground. The scent of wet leaves and pine surrounded him. He pushed aside some tree branches with the length of his rifle. The brush was thick and difficult to navigate, leaving him with a claustrophobic feeling. His heart beat increased. Adrenaline and fear narrowed his vision. It took several deep breaths to clear it.

The dog halted suddenly. Everyone froze. Wally's history with bombs meant the area surrounding the cabin could be booby-trapped, hence the bomb detection dogs with every team. Jackson held his breath. Sweat beaded on his brow, mixing with the rain before dripping down the side of his face.

Lisa pressed forward. Her handler gave the okay signal with his hand and Jackson took more steps forward. The cabin came into view. It was in a natural valley. Firewood lined the front porch and a rustic rocking chair sat discarded on the grass. This place had once belonged to Wally and Todd's maternal grandfather. The deed had never been updated, which explained why it hadn't come up during a property search.

The team commander gave the hand signal showing they should spread out. Jackson moved to the left, as designated. It was slow trekking, the foliage thick and green.

A blast erupted, white-hot heat and debris flew as the house exploded. Flames sparked in the trees. The force of the bomb nearly knocked Jackson off his feet. He struggled to draw in a breath, the air tinged with ash.

Suddenly, movement snagged his attention. He caught a flash of color as a man took off running.

Wally.

Jackson hit the button on his intercom. "I've got Wally. He's running northbound, headed for the road. I'm in pursuit."

There was no response. Were the comms down? Taken offline by the explosion?

Jackson didn't waste any time to find out. He bolted through the trees. Branches smacked his face. His breath came in bursts, the bulletproof vest and the tactical gear weighing him down. Sweat poured down his back. He tripped, nearly face-planting, but caught himself at the last moment.

Wally disappeared around a bend. Jackson kept going. He tried to keep the other man in sight without risking his own life. There was no way to know if Wally was armed. Or if he was leading him into another trap. Roots threatened to trip Jackson again and thick tree branches hindered his view.

Wally reached a dirt path and then whirled.

Jackson ducked.

A bullet winged over his head and lodged into a tree. He gritted his teeth. "Texas Ranger! You're surrounded, Wally. Drop your weapon and put your hands on your head."

The criminal ignored him. Wally fired a few more rounds before taking off into the woods. If he had a plan, it wasn't obvious.

Jackson updated his status to the team in case the comms were working and then continued in pursuit. He couldn't lose Wally. Piper's life depended on it. Heart pounding and anxiety swirling his insides, Jackson followed Wally's path uphill. He kept his rifle at the ready and his gaze sharp, searching for any sign of an ambush. The nighttime animals were silent. Even they knew there was a predator nearby.

A drop-off appeared out of nowhere. Jackson windmilled his arms back to prevent momentum from taking him over the edge. Air whistled across the bare skin of his neck. He had just one heartbeat to steady himself before Wally slammed into him.

They crashed to the ground. Cold mud sank into the fabric of Jackson's clothes. By the grace of God, Wally's gun clattered down the side of the cliff. He was no longer armed, but that didn't stop the assault. Jackson struggled to get the upper hand, but with the tactical gear weighing him down, hand-to-hand combat was ineffective. Wally was strong and wiry and able to move much faster.

They struggled over control of the rifle. Wally's expression was fierce and determined. Death shone in his eyes. There would be no forgiveness if he disarmed Jackson. The criminal would kill him without blinking.

Jackson elbowed Wally in the throat. The man gagged, his grip loosening on the rifle, but then he reared back and hit Jackson in the face with a heavy rock.

An explosion of light and pain blasted across his cheek, blinding him. A kick to the shin followed. Jackson grabbed Wally's foot when he went for round two and twisted. The criminal crashed to the ground. The rock came around again. This time, it glanced off Jackson's helmet, but the hit was delivered with enough force to rattle his teeth.

He aimed his rifle at Wally. "Don't move, or I'll shoot you."

Wally froze. His breath came in pants. The rain increased in tempo, the downpour soaking both men instantly. Thunder rumbled. Jackson kept his rifle trained on the criminal. "Drop the rock and put your hands on your head."

His words had to be shouted to be heard over the rain. Wally didn't move. Jackson could see he was calculating his next move. For half a moment, he thought Wally was going to rush him.

Then Daniel stepped out of the woods, his own rifle trained on Wally. "Drop the rock and put your hands behind head."

Grady followed. Surrounded and with little choice, Wally did as he was instructed. When the handcuffs were slapped on his wrists, Jackson breathed a sigh of relief. "Todd?"

"Nowhere to be found." Daniel lowered his rifle and extended a hand. "You hurt?"

"I'll survive." Jackson waved off the help and rose. Muscles he hadn't known he had were aching. Blood dripped from the wound on his cheek. He winced when Daniel shone a light on it.

"That's gonna need stitches."

Jackson didn't care. What mattered was Piper's safety. He focused on Wally. "Where's your brother?"

"I want a lawyer."

He growled. "I bet you do." He started to take a step forward, but the muddy ground underneath him gave way. His stomach bottomed out.

Then he was airborne as a mud slide took him down the cliff.

TWENTY-FIVE

Piper nursed a cup of coffee and watched the dawn break. The clouds parted just enough to allow rays of golden light to spread across the backyard. Moxie rested at her feet, as if he instinctually understood she needed comfort. Right now, Jackson and the rest of the team were raiding the Hutchinsons' cabin. It was a dangerous mission fraught with complications. Her mind wanted to engage in what-ifs, each possibility worse than the last, until she purposefully drove the thoughts away.

She wouldn't think the worst. It was an occupational hazard—law enforcement officers were trained to analyze every possibility—but that wasn't helpful now. It would only ramp up her anxiety and make her stir-crazy. Instead, she leaned into prayer, hoping the Good Lord would ease her troubled heart.

"Good morning, baby girl. You're up early." Grandma Mary shuffled into the kitchen. She wore a robe and slippers. A brightly colored scarf was wrapped around her head to protect her hair while sleeping.

"Jackson called. They've started the raid."

"Ah." Grandma Mary bowed her head and whispered a quick prayer before hugging Piper. "God will see them through." She kissed Piper's forehead. "How about some breakfast to go with that coffee? Otherwise, you'll have stomach pains on top of your troubles."

"I don't know if I can eat."

"Well, I'll whip up a batch of my famous French toast and then we'll see." Grandma Mary grinned and then glanced around the kitchen. "Where's Cole? I'm surprised he's not up with you."

"He's doing a perimeter check."

"Well I know he'll be hungry. I'll make a double batch."

She gathered ingredients from the fridge and hummed a tune while mixing the eggs. Piper was instantly transported back to her childhood. She'd spent hours with Grandma Mary in the kitchen, doing her schoolwork while cookies were baking or a lasagna was being assembled. Those small moments were some of her happiest times.

Grandma Mary hadn't had the easiest life. Like Piper and Ava, she'd grown up in an abusive household. She met the love of her life at twenty-five and was happily married for almost three decades before a car accident took her husband. They'd never had children—fertility problems—so the couple opened their home to foster kids.

Piper twisted the coffee mug in her hands. "Grandma Mary, can I ask you something?"

"Anything, baby girl."

"Do you think some people are so damaged it's better for them to avoid marriage?" She bit her lip. "I worry that I'll drag Jackson down with all my issues. He's so loyal and dedicated, he'll never admit when it's too much."

"Why do you assume it will ever be too much for him?"

"It's too much for me sometimes. I can't imagine it won't be too much for Jackson."

"That's because you try to carry the burden alone, baby girl." Grandma Mary abandoned her cooking and pulled out a chair next to Piper. "We aren't meant to walk this world on our own. Do you think it's a coincidence Jackson was assigned this case? No. It's divine providence. God brought you and Jackson back together again because He knows what you have is special. Neither of you had forgotten the other. The love you built as teenagers has grown deeper and stronger, and Jackson has bravely followed his heart. He keeps reaching for you and does so knowing there's a risk you'll push him away again."

"I thought I was protecting Jackson by pushing him away."

"No, baby girl. You're not helping him now and you didn't help him ten years ago. You only prolonged the suffering. You were hurting, and he was hurting. Trouble was, neither of you could comfort the other."

Piper let that sink in. "Ava told me Jackson called you for months after the attack."

"He loves you. Deeply. And Jackson has the strength to support you, but he can't do it if you fight him every step of the way." Grandma Mary placed a hand on her arm. "I know it's scary. As a child, you learned not to rely on the adults in your life because they weren't there for you. But you aren't that scared little girl anymore. You can put your trust in God. He speaks to your heart. Follow his guidance and you'll never go wrong."

It was excellent advice. Wasn't Piper's biggest regret leaving Jackson behind when she left ten years ago? She'd known in her heart it was a mistake, but she'd ignored it. Her past didn't have to be her future though. God had given her a second chance with the man she loved. She could choose differently this time.

Piper hugged Grandma Mary. "Thank you."

"Anytime, baby girl."

"Good morning." Ava stood in the doorway and yawned. She was still in her pajamas but didn't look like she'd slept a wink. Piper knew her sister was worried about Derek. "Why do you two look so serious?"

"We were having a discussion about God and accepting His divine intervention."

Ava grinned. "Were you? I got that lecture yesterday."

"Excuse me, I do not lecture." Grandma Mary rose and went back to the stove, flipping on the burner underneath the skillet. "I advise. Sometimes the discussion is more forceful, but you can be a stubborn lot."

Ava and Piper laughed.

Then Ava's expression grew serious. "Any word?"

"No." Piper rose and poured her sister a cup of coffee. "I'm sure Derek or Jackson will call as soon as they can." Her lips lifted and she wagged her brows. "What is the official status of your relationship? You kissed and had a chat in his office, but I haven't heard a peep from you since then."

Ava blushed and sipped her coffee. "We're together." She held out a hand. "We'll take it slow, for the kids' sake. I want to give them time to get used to the idea, but... I love him. I've loved him for a long time."

Piper whooped and hugged her sister. "I'm so happy for you both."

The scent of French toast filled the kitchen. Piper busied herself by setting the table and absently listened to Ava and Grandma Mary chat. Her mind was still on the earlier conversation. Was it that easy? Just accept the love being given her? Maybe it was.

Her cell phone rang. Piper retrieved it from the counter and her heart stuttered. It was the killer. Her finger hesitated over the button, but then she hit accept, stepping into the laundry room so Grandma Mary and Ava wouldn't overhear the conversation. "What do you want?"

"Good morning to you too." The distorted voice sent a shiver down Piper's spine. "I called to say your little plan didn't work. I warned you this wasn't Wally, but you persisted, and now you're no closer to figuring out my identity."

"So why don't you just tell me who you are?"

"And ruin all the fun? No, Piper. I want to see your face when my identity is finally revealed to you."

This sicko was getting a thrill out of playing games with her. She gripped the phone tighter, glancing out into the backyard. Cole was nowhere to be found. She left the laundry room and hurried to the front of the house. "If you and I come face-to-face, I promise it'll be a decision you regret."

He laughed. "Always so tough, aren't you? But I know how to break you, Piper."

Her heart stuttered. She spotted Cole in the driveway on his cell phone. Concern was etched across his face. Anxiety swirled and bile rose in the back of her throat. Jackson. Something happened to Jackson. She gritted her teeth. "What did you do?"

"I took care of a problem. See you soon."

He hung up. With trembling fingers, Piper flipped open the locks, grabbing her car keys and gun before stepping outside. The crisp morning air cooled her heated cheeks and a drizzle dampened her clothes. She hurried to Cole. "What happened to Jackson?"

"You shouldn't be outside."

He took her elbow, but she yanked it away. Piper knew she was being rude but couldn't make herself care. All that mattered was Jackson. She glared at Cole. "What happened?"

"He was injured during the operation and is being transported to the hospital—"

She didn't need to hear any more. Piper raced to her vehicle. Cole called her name, tried to intervene, but she was too quick. Within seconds, she peeled out of the driveway.

A patrol car was stationed at the end of the road. She slowed down long enough to instruct the officer behind the wheel to follow her to the hospital. She needed to get to Jackson, but she wasn't reckless. The killer had called for a reason. He wanted to get her alone. Did he plan to stage an accident to grab her? Possibly. She wouldn't take the chance.

Piper turned on her turret lights and hit the gas. Familiar landmarks whipped past. She gripped the steering wheel, unable to do anything but focus on the road ahead. God knew what was in her heart. He heard her silent cries. Soon, the hospital appeared. Piper slowed down and turned into the parking lot. She waved the deputy forward. When his vehicle lined up with hers, she lowered her window. "Go back to the house. I'll be okay from here."

"You sure, Detective?"

"Yes." There were cameras in the parking lot and the hospital was a few steps away. People mingled in a nearby cafe, despite the early morning hour. Piper nodded to the deputy. "Thanks for the assistance."

He gave a wave and drove off. She parked her car. Thunder rumbled as she ran across the lot. All she wanted was to get to Jackson. How badly was he injured? A thousand horrors flashed through her mind before she could push them away, but the panic remained. She loved him. Needed him. *Please, God, please watch over him.*

Suddenly, a truck flew out of a parking spot as she was walking behind and rammed into her.

Pain exploded along her right leg from the collision. She was airborne for a few seconds as momentum tossed her across the parking lot onto the hood of another car. A crack resounded in her elbow as it collided with the windshield. White-hot agony followed. Blinding pain, unlike any she'd ever experienced. Her body slid off the hood of the car onto the ground. Her head rapped against the bumper and stars appeared in her vision.

Somewhere inside her head, a voice was screaming for her to run, but Piper couldn't get her body to cooperate. She blinked, trying to clear her vision. So much pain. It stole her breath. Blackness edged her vision.

In the next moment, she was lifted. Piper screamed. Every move sent more pain through her. The blackness beckoned. She struggled to fight against it, but when her body was dumped into the back seat of a vehicle, it was more than she could take.

She lost consciousness.

TWENTY-SIX

Jackson held still while the plastic surgeon stitched the gash on his cheek. The mud slide had carried him several feet before he was pushed to the side. It was a miracle he survived. Since arriving at the hospital, he'd gotten a full work-up. MRI scan, blood work, and a dose of IV antibiotics. Apparently, open wounds and mud didn't go well together.

Jackson's injuries were thankfully minor, but the entire process had taken hours. His cell phone was somewhere at the bottom of the valley in a heap of mud. Calling Piper was impossible. To make matters worse, the emergency room was packed. No one from the ranger team was allowed in Jackson's curtained-off area. He prayed someone—like Derek or Grady—had the foresight to call and let Piper know he was all right. Otherwise, she'd be frantic.

"Almost done." The doctor spread ointment and then added a bandage.

Jackson barely felt any of it. His cheek was numb from the local anesthetic. He listened as the doctor gave care instructions. The wound wouldn't scar, not that Jackson cared much, and he'd need oral antibiotics for the next week. Then the nurse came in with his discharge papers.

With a sigh of relief, Jackson strolled out of the curtained area into the hall. His borrowed clothes—Daniel had given them to a nurse—were a touch too tight, the pants an inch too short, but at least they were clean. He was eager to call Piper. Cole was keeping an eye on her, and he knew his colleague would keep her safe, but Jackson would feel much better after hearing her voice.

He rounded the corner to the exit. Daniel and Lieutenant Rodriguez were coming from the opposite direction and nearly plowed into him. Jackson screeched to a stop, quickly registering the worry in their expressions. If a doctor or nurse had allowed them past the main doors to the emergency room, something was very wrong. His heart skittered. "What is it?"

"Piper was kidnapped from the hospital parking lot." Lieutenant Rodriguez's voice was blunt, but her expression held sympathy. "She was hit by a truck, and while injured, taken by a masked man."

Jackson nearly bowled over at the news. He didn't know which part was worse. "She was hit?" He swallowed hard. "What was she doing here?"

"Apparently, she learned you'd been injured. She dodged Cole's attempt to stop her, jumped in her vehicle, and raced over. Piper had a police escort to the hospital but dismissed the deputy once she arrived in the parking lot. She probably figured with the cameras and so many people around, she was safe."

She'd been coming for him. Jackson had known she would. Piper loved deeply, and whenever someone she cared about needed her, she raced right to their side. It was one of the many reasons he loved her.

"As she was crossing the lot, a truck pulled right out of a parking space," Vikki continued. "Piper had no time to react."

Daniel nodded in agreement with their boss. "The truck belongs to Wally and although the man was masked, we believe it's Todd Hutchinson."

Of course. Who else could it be?

Jackson gritted his teeth against the rising sense of panic. Had Todd taken her in an attempt to save his brother? Or was Piper in the hands of a killer? Both options were horrific, and his mind filled with frightening images. Jackson pushed them away. He needed to focus on the one thing that mattered: saving the love of his life. "I want to interview Wally. Where is he?"

"He's conferring with counsel, but so far, we've been unable to convince his attorney to let him talk to us." Lieutenant Rodriguez pegged him with a look. "His lawyer is Shawn. I know you have a personal relationship with him and that could work to our advantage. But do you think you can handle being in the same room with Wally and keep your cool?"

Jackson didn't hesitate. "Absolutely. Piper's life depends on it."

Vikki eyed him for another moment as if gauging his sincerity. He met her gaze straight on. After several beats, she nodded. "Take Daniel with you. I'm going to continue coordinating the search efforts. Let me know immediately if you learn anything that can help."

"Yes, ma'am."

Jackson followed Daniel to the elevators. The doors swished closed, and for a moment, he was transported back to the talk he'd had with Piper right here in this very cabin. His words haunted him. "I told Piper about Company A. About how nearly everyone met their significant other under dangerous circumstances. That every one of those women nearly died. I explained the odds weren't with us. Sometime, someone in Company A was going to be on the losing end of this equation and..." His voice grew thick. "I didn't want it to be me."

Daniel placed a hand on his shoulder in brotherly solidarity. "Have faith, man. None of us are giving up on finding Piper, and you shouldn't either. Screw the odds. Piper is strong. She's survived things that would break other people. If anyone can get through this, it's her."

Jackson sucked in a deep breath to settle his runaway emotions. "You're right. I just..."

"Needed a moment. Yeah, I get it." Daniel squeezed his shoulder and then released it. "What you and Piper have is special. It's obvious to anyone who sees you two together. If my ex-wife and I had loved each other like that, we wouldn't have gotten divorced."

Daniel rarely spoke about his divorce. Jackson only knew it'd happened a long time ago. Whatever the cause, it'd scarred his colleague. Daniel never dated or expressed a romantic interest in anyone. It was as if that part of his life was over.

The elevator dinged, and the doors opened. Deputies were stationed outside Wally's hospital room. Jackson greeted them with a flash of his badge. "Is his attorney still here?" Since he'd invoked his right to counsel, law enforcement couldn't question Wally without his attorney present. A deputy confirmed Shawn was inside the hospital room. Jackson knocked and then entered.

Shock rippled through him as Shawn's wife, Melanie, turned to face him. Wally was seated behind her, wearing a hospital gown. Both of his hands were cuffed to the bed, and a sneer formed on his lips at the sight of Jackson.

Jackson ignored him, focusing on Melanie. "Where's Shawn?"

"He was called away for an urgent matter. You can deal with me. I'm a partner with Kingston Law Firm now."

Shock was then followed quickly by suspicion. It burned bright and hot. Piper was kidnapped, and Shawn suddenly disappeared. This case had revolved around Elena and Shawn's affair from the beginning. But then why would Shawn send them to the cabin?

Jackson's stomach twisted as a horrible thought bubbled up in his mind. What if Wally was supposed to blow up the cabin with a bunch of law enforcement officers inside it? People would be injured. Even if Jackson wasn't, Piper knew many of the members of the team. She'd come to the hospital to show support.

This whole elaborate setup was designed to separate her from Jackson and then lure her to the hospital.

And it had worked.

Melanie's bright red mouth made a moue of dissatisfaction. "Our client has nothing to say to law enforcement."

"That's fine. He can just listen." Jackson pegged Wally with a steely gaze. Todd was the ringleader. It was the only thing that made sense. Wally was a pawn used by his brother as a distraction. Jackson was taking a risk with the tactic running through his mind, but it felt right and fit with the evidence they knew, so he ran with it. "The situation has changed. Detective Piper Jensen has been kidnapped by your brother. Unlike your brother, you haven't killed anyone yet. The minute Detective Jensen dies though, Wally, your situation gets infinitely worse."

Wally locked his jaw, but underneath the sheet, his leg jittered. He was uncomfortable.

"Texas jurors don't like killers. If you know where Todd has taken Detective Jensen and you conceal it from us, I can guarantee the state's attorney will throw the book at you. There's not a jury in the world that will take a look at your criminal history and believe you're innocent of these crimes. Especially when we get your girlfriends on the stand. Remember Kylie? The mother of your child? The woman you beat badly enough she went to the hospital. Twice."

Melanie's cheeks heated. "Don't threaten—"

"Oh, it's not a threat, ma'am. It's a promise." Jackson

practically shook with rage, but he contained his anger, and kept his gaze locked on Wally. He softened his voice. "But there's a way to make this all go away. We can't prove, yet, that you blew up the cabin. We can't prove you killed anyone. Maybe it's a misunderstanding. If you help us find Detective Jensen, then it's possible you won't spend a night in jail."

"That's ridiculous." Melanie sputtered. "Wally, don't listen to him—"

"I wanna talk."

Jackson's heart skipped a beat, and he stepped toward Wally. "Do you revoke your right to counsel?"

"No, he doesn't," Melanie snapped. "Wally, he's trying to trick you."

Wally sat forward, the cuffs on his wrists holding him back as he strained toward her. "Are you stupid? Do you think I'm going to prison over this! I told my brother this was a bad idea, and he didn't listen to me. Now I'm the one who's going to pay the price while he walks around a free man."

"You have to revoke your right to counsel," Jackson interjected. "Do you?"

"Yes." Wally nodded. "I don't want her in here. Get her out!"

Daniel grabbed Melanie's elbow and steered her toward the door. "You heard the man. Let's go."

She protested loudly and continued doing so even as Daniel gently pushed her into the hall. He shut the door and locked it.

Wally panted like he'd run a marathon. Sweat

beaded on his forehead and his heart rate monitor was flying. Jackson feared the older man would have a heart attack before he could tell them anything.

"It's okay. She's gone." Jackson hated the soothing tone he was forced to use, but keeping Wally on their side was essential. Every minute that ticked by with Piper in Todd's grasp made her situation all that more precarious.

"I need protection." Wally's eyes were wide, as if he couldn't quite believe he'd thrown his attorney out of the room. "I'll tell you what I know, but I want protection. A new name, a new life far away from here."

Fear oozed from his pores and his leg jittered harder underneath the bed. Sweat stains appeared on the hospital gown.

"Who do you want protection from?" Jackson asked. "Your brother?"

Wally laughed. It was low and guttural, and sounded like he'd smoked a thousand cigarettes. "Todd would never hurt me. We're family. I protected him from our dad and Todd worships the ground I walk on." His gaze met Jackson's. "I need protection from someone bigger than Todd." His attention shot to the door and then back to Jackson. "Get me a deal and I'll talk. Tell you every-thing, including where Todd is taking Detective Jensen."

"Tell us where she is now."

"I'm not that dumb," Wally sneered. "The minute I do that, you'll throw me in jail. The detective is my ticket out of this mess. But the clock is ticking. Melanie won't wait long."

Jackson's blood ran ice cold. "You need protection from Shawn."

Not a flicker of acknowledgment showed on Wally's face. Jackson couldn't tell if he was afraid of Shawn or not.

"Get me a deal," Wally said. "Or Detective Jensen dies."

TWENTY-SEVEN

Someone was yelling.

Piper's eyes drifted open, and she winced as the light hit her irises. Pain radiated out from her chest. Every breath was excruciating. Confusion muddled her brain. She processed things in slow motion. Leather. She was sprawled across a leather couch. Cool air washed across her cheek from a vent above her. The carpeting on the floor was thick and plush, the color of a clear summer sky. A short distance away stood a pair of legs. They were clad in dirty jeans and expensive tennis shoes.

Todd Hutchinson.

With a jolt, Piper remembered getting hit by the truck. Being placed in the extended cab. That's why every inch of her body hurt. Judging from the way her chest ached, she had a broken rib or two. The pain was washed away by a rush of adrenaline as fear took hold.

She battled against it. At the moment, Todd was facing away from her. He hadn't noticed she was awake.

It was a small consolation, but it gave Piper a moment to fully assess how bad the situation was. Then she nearly laughed out loud. She'd been kidnapped by a sadistic serial killer. It didn't get much worse.

"I didn't tell you to bring her here!"

The voice was fueled with rage and frustration. Piper's gaze slipped toward the window on the far side of the room. She inhaled sharply in surprise, sending a bolt of pain arcing from her ribs.

Standing on the other side of the home office was Paul Kingston. His face was mottled with fury, gaze locked on Todd. "Do you understand how police investigations work? She's bleeding all over my couch! My carpet! Not to mention that a neighbor could have seen your truck driving in the neighborhood. The sheriff's department already suspects my son is involved. It wouldn't be a leap for them to suspect me too."

"But they don't. You told me yourself." Todd's tone was calm and controlled. He'd changed his appearance, probably to avoid detection by law enforcement. His head was shaved, and he'd grown a beard. "Your contact in the sheriff's department has kept you informed. I know you're aware my brother has been arrested. Nothing will go according to plan until you figure out a way to get Wally out of this."

"Your brother blew up a cabin with law enforcement nearby. He's not getting out of this anytime soon." Paul jabbed a finger in Todd's direction. "You should've kept him out of it. In fact, you were supposed to take the money and leave after Elena was killed. You've created this mess!"

Todd stalked closer to Paul. "No one knew about that cabin except me, Wally, and you. So how did law enforcement find out about it?"

Paul threw up his hands. "I don't know. Maybe Wally told his girlfriend about it? Deputies have interviewed her several times."

"No. My brother has never trusted women."

The energy pouring off Todd was palpable. His expression was controlled, his voice calm, but Piper sensed it wouldn't last. Like a panther sneaking up on its prey, Todd was deadly. Paul didn't realize what a precarious position he was in.

Thankfully, the two men were paying attention to each other and not her. She shifted her weight slowly and agony swept up her arm. Her left elbow was swollen and horribly bruised. Broken? Likely. She gritted her teeth and tried to push into a sitting position. That made the pain in her chest explode. Darkness clouded her vision. She was in bad shape. *God, please help me. Give me strength.*

Paul noticed her slight movements and his face flushed an even deeper shade of red. He pointed. "Look! Now she's awake."

Todd turned, and a smile lifted the corners of his lips. His gaze swept over her with a hunger that sent ice running through Piper's veins. Her breath stalled. This. This was the real Todd Hutchinson. The man she'd interviewed before the bombing was an alter ego, carefully crafted to make Todd appear like a disorganized and sloppy alcoholic. It was a clever ruse to keep anyone from suspecting his true nature.

A cold-blooded killer.

She met his gaze. Her throat was dry and her lips cracked, but she managed to croak out, "You murdered Elena. And Gerdie."

Todd laughed. "Finally. Although I must say, Piper, I'm disappointed. I thought you'd figure out it was me much earlier."

She hadn't. Not really. Jackson had seen through Todd from the start though.

Jackson. Her throat clogged, and tears pricked her eyes at the thought of him. Was he still alive, or had he succumbed to his injuries from the cabin bombing? Even if she survived this—which was unlikely—Piper still might not get the chance to answer the question he'd posed to her last night. He didn't know she was ready to stay and fight for their love.

Regret and sorrow threatened to drown her. Piper forced it back. As long as she was still breathing, there was hope. She'd run away from Jackson too many times. She wouldn't do it again. Not physically, mentally, or emotionally. Fighting for their life together started now.

"You need to get her out of here," Paul ordered, reigniting the argument between him and Todd. "This wasn't the plan. You've mucked things up from the beginning. If you had just taken the money and left town as we planned, then none of this would've happened."

Piper's mind whirled. She suddenly understood that

Paul had hired Todd to kill Elena. They'd suspected Shawn, but they were wrong.

Todd snarled. "I'm not going through with anything until you figure out a way to get my brother out of this mess."

Once again, the men were focused on each other. Piper scanned the surrounding area. She needed a weapon. The small table next to her held books and a magazine. Nothing helpful. Bookshelves lined one wall. A few paperweights were used as decor, but there was no way to know how heavy they were. Or if she could lift them. To her shock, Todd hadn't restrained her. Maybe he thought the injuries she'd suffered from being hit by the truck would keep her from moving quickly.

He wasn't wrong. Every part of her hurt when she breathed.

Paul puffed out his chest and stepped closer to Todd. "Wally shouldn't have gotten involved. That stunt he pulled with Marcus? It was reckless and stupid. You were supposed to manage him. It's not my fault that he got himself caught."

"It is your fault. No one knew about the cabin. You told the cops."

"No, I didn't." Paul's ire increased, along with the volume of his voice. "Don't forget who you're dealing with. I know all of your secrets. The crimes you've committed, the women you've killed. Do you want me to start sharing information with law enforcement?"

With the grace and speed of a professional boxer, Todd's fist slammed into Paul's face. The crack of cartilage proceeded a blast of blood and a howl of pain. Paul bent over, and Todd took advantage by smashing his fist a second time into the older man's face. Then he grabbed him by the scruff of his blood-stained shirt and shoved him against the wall.

Todd leaned over Paul. "You made a deal with the devil, old man, and you know what they say, the devil always gets his due. I killed Elena and I have the receipts tying you to the murder. Do you want me to give those to the police?"

Paul wheezed in response.

"My brother protected me from our dad when I was a kid," Todd continued. "I'm going to stay loyal to him. So I don't care what you need to do, but you're getting Wally out of this."

Paul held up his hands in surrender. "Okay."

Todd smirked and punched him again in the gut. "Don't threaten me again."

The violence was brutal. Was this a sample of what Elena and Gerdie had gone through? Is this what Todd was planning on doing to her? Piper's heart rate spiked. Fear tasted sour in her mouth and her breath came in short pants. She couldn't even draw in full breaths to counteract the adrenaline coursing through her. She pulled air in through her nose and held it for three seconds before letting it out. Then she did it again.

A flash of metal caught her attention. Piper winced as she stuck the fingers of her right hand in between the couch cushions, and they brushed against something hard. She tugged it free.

A letter opener. It had a sharp point and an intricate handle engraved with lady justice.

Thank you, sweet God in Heaven.

The blade was short and not very sharp. It didn't guarantee her survival, but it was a weapon. It was a chance. Piper just needed to wait for the right moment.

Paul lay on the ground with Todd standing over him. He pushed himself into a sitting position. Blood coated the lower half of his face and stained his clothes. He spat a tooth onto the carpet. "You broke my nose."

"I'm gonna break a lot more than your nose." Todd grabbed Paul by his shirt and lifted him to his feet, hurrying him over to the desk chair. "Call the governor. Call a senator. I don't care who you call, but you need to get the charges against my brother dropped now."

Piper couldn't believe what she was witnessing. Did Todd really believe that Paul could get Wally out of criminal charges simply by placing a phone call? It wasn't going to happen. Which, it seemed, Paul already knew. But now that he'd taken a beating from Todd, he was desperate to figure out how to get away from him.

Paul held up his hands. "I need a few minutes to think."

"You've got two."

Todd shifted his attention to Piper. His gaze was predatory. Blood-thirsty.

Bile rose in the back of her throat as he stalked closer. She wanted to sink back into the couch but resisted. Fear was Todd's drug. He fed off of it, craved it. She wouldn't give him a drop. Instead, she jutted up her chin and met his gaze with one of her own. "You won't get away with this."

He chuckled. "I have so far." Todd reached the couch. He trailed a finger along the curve of Piper's cheek and it took every bit of willpower not to shudder at the contact. "I wanted you from the beginning, but you always thought you were too good for me. You preferred Jackson, a weak-willed moron, when you could've had a real man. I thought when Lionel attacked you, it would kill my obsession, but it never went away. You've haunted me."

In a flash, his hand wrapped around her throat. Piper's heart rate spiked. His fingers constricted her airflow, and his body crushed her already damaged ribs. She nearly passed out from the pain alone. Todd hovered above her. His eyes were dark pools of hatred. "I knew you ran along the path in the nature preserve. Elena was a preview. I shot her and made her run toward you, so you could see what was coming."

He lightened the pressure on her throat. Piper sucked in a tiny bit of air. Her fingers were locked around the letter opener. She wanted to wait for the right moment, but if Todd choked her enough that she passed out and then moved her while she was unconscious, she'd lose her chance to get away.

He chuckled. "I'm gonna have so much fun with you." Then he growled and squeezed her throat again. His shoulders dropped as he added pressure.

Piper's vision narrowed. She had one shot at this.

Without warning, and faster than she could've

believed possible considering her injuries, she jabbed the letter opener into Todd's neck. He screamed as the blade wedged deep into his skin. Blood spurted from the wound. The pressure on her throat immediately eased as Todd jumped back. Piper sucked in a much-needed breath. Her ribs screamed in protest.

Todd, red-faced and panicked, held his fingers to the wound. Piper had aimed for his artery. It wasn't clear if her aim had been accurate. Fear propelled her to her feet. At best, she'd mortally wounded him. At worst, she'd enraged him. She wouldn't wait to find out which one it was.

On shaky steps, she stumbled for the door. Paul didn't make a move to stop her. He gaped openmouthed at Todd, as if he couldn't believe this was happening in his home office. Under other circumstances, the expression on his face was comical, but now, it was simply a relief. She wouldn't have to fight off two men in her condition.

Piper yanked open the office door. The house was a mansion on a wide expanse of property. Was there a housekeeping staff? Gardeners? Not everyone who worked for Paul was crooked, right? Then again, if Todd was merely injured, he would kill anyone who attempted to help her.

She limped down the hallway. Her left leg had been badly bruised in the collision with the truck and screamed with pain. Adrenaline masked some of it. Behind her, in the office, she heard Todd bellow her name. It was coarse and wild. Like a monster being unleashed.

Her breath came in pants as she rounded the corner into an expansive living room. Couches were arranged around an elegant coffee table. A hutch along one wall. Todd's footsteps pounded behind her.

The sound of glass breaking erupted from different parts of the house. A second later, smoke filled the room.

Hope alighted in Piper's heart. Jackson and the ranger team had figured out where she was. The SWAT team was preparing to enter, but the place was massive and it would take time to search. Todd was obsessed. He wouldn't let her go easily, not even under these circumstances.

He screamed her name again, and his footsteps drew closer.

Piper dropped to her knees and maneuvered to the hutch. She opened a door, grateful to find the cabinet was empty. She crawled inside. Silent prayers exited her lips. Her breath came in pants, and it felt like her heart was about to explode out of her chest. Tears, from fear and from the smoke, streamed down her face.

She didn't know who would find her first.

Her comrades?

Or Todd?

TWENTY-EIGHT

Three days later, Jackson paced the length of the hospital corridor. He had to keep moving. It was that or fall over from exhaustion. He'd been running on caffeine and worry ever since Piper was brought to the emergency room. Those first several hours, when she was in surgery, were harrowing. She'd nearly died.

He didn't like to think about it.

Grandma Mary emerged from the hospital room. The last few days had put her through the wringer too. Weariness was etched in the wrinkles on her face, but she gave him a bright smile. "She's dressed. You can go in." Mary adjusted the shoulder strap on her purse. "I'm heading home for some much needed rest. I suggest you two do the same once the nurse returns with her discharge paperwork."

"We will, but first we have a meeting at the sheriff's department."

Her mouth pursed in disapproval.

Jackson sensed a good-natured lecture coming on and he quickly added, "I tried to talk Piper out of it. She insisted. Rest will come a lot easier once she has the answers to her questions."

Mary's expression softened. "I suppose that's true." She reached into her purse and pulled out a small jewelry box. "I brought something for you."

Jackson frowned and accepted the offering. He opened the box to find a stunning diamond ring nestled inside. His breath hitched.

"This was my engagement ring," Mary said. "Perhaps I'm jumping the gun, but I'd got the impression you were going to ask Piper to marry you. She's always loved this piece. I stopped wearing it a few years ago because of my arthritis and wasn't sure what to do with it. But God, as always, had a plan. I'd be honored if you'd consider using it."

Jackson was moved beyond words. "It's perfect." He hugged the older woman, his heart full of joy and love. "Thank you. It means more than I can say." Nerves jittered his insides. "Piper and I haven't spoken about our future. Not really. I'm not sure we're on the same page."

"Never mind." She patted his cheek. "Keep the ring anyway. If you don't need it, you can give it back."

She turned and strolled down the hallway. Jackson watched her go for a moment and then stared down at the stunning ring. It was a vintage piece with smaller stones surrounding a larger diamond. He could easily see it on Piper's finger. It was just her style.

Marriage. It would be a dream come true, but

broaching the subject might cause trouble. For the last few days, Piper's focus had been on recovering from her injuries. Jackson stayed by her side, and she seemed grateful for his support, but that was a far cry from forever.

God, I leave it in Your hands. Show me the right time to tell Piper what's in my heart.

The prayer gave him peace. Jackson closed the jewelry box and slipped it into his pocket. Then he entered the hospital room. His breath stalled. Piper was sitting in the chair next to the window. Sunlight streamed over the glossy strands of her hair and across the delicate curve of her cheek. Her silk button-up blouse brought out the natural rosy hue of her cheeks. She was stunning.

She faced him and smiled. His heart clenched. "Hey, beautiful."

Piper scoffed. She absently touched the purple bruises along her throat. "Hardly. It's a shame we aren't closer to Halloween. Ava could put me in a lawn chair in the front yard to scare the neighbors."

Jackson smiled at her self-deprecating humor. "I was thinking you could be a superhero for Halloween this year. Piper the Invincible. Brave enough to stand her ground against serial killers and the lawyers who protect them." He brushed a tender kiss across her mouth, mindful of her injuries. "We'll need to find a letter opener though."

She laughed and then winced.

He pushed a strand of hair behind her ear. "Need some pain medication?"

"No, I don't like the way it makes me feel. I'll stick to the over-the-counter stuff from now on."

A cast covered her left arm, and she had her leg propped up on the bed. Her injuries were shockingly minor compared to how bad things could have been. Some broken ribs, a shattered elbow, and a bruised femur were the highlights.

Jackson perched on the window ledge next to her. "Are you sure you're up to visiting the sheriff's department today? We can easily get an update when you've had more time to recover."

She shook her head. "No. I want to do it today." Piper reached for his hand, sliding her fingers between his. "Let's close this chapter, so we can move on with the rest of our lives."

His brows arched playfully, even as his heart rate sped up. "The rest of our lives, huh?"

She blushed and smiled. "Is that too forward? Oh, well." She gently tugged him down until they were face-to-face. Piper stared him in the eyes as if she was memorizing the moment. "I love you, Jackson Barker, and I'm ready to walk..." Her lips quirked. "Actually, limp, into the future with you. I'm done running. No more pushing you away. Whatever problems arise, we'll face them together. I don't promise it will be easy, but I swear to fight for us. Always."

His throat clogged with emotion. It was the most wonderful thing anyone had ever said to him. For the second time in ten minutes, Jackson found himself moved beyond words.

Now. His heart said now was the moment.

Jackson bent down on one knee.

Piper gasped and her eyes widened. "What are you doing?"

"I'm taking advantage of the moment quickly before you change your mind." He removed the jewelry box from his pocket and took her hand in his. "Piper Jensen, I have loved you from the first moment I saw you, strolling down the high school hallway with an apple in one hand, a chemistry book in the other, and a fierce determination to live your dreams. You stole my breath away. And just now, you did it again."

Her chin trembled. Tears shimmered in her beautiful eyes.

"I don't know what the future holds, but I know my love for you is forever." With trembling fingers, Jackson opened the jewelry box. "Will you marry me?"

"Yes!"

There was no hesitation in her answer, and Piper didn't even bother to look at the engagement ring. She threw her arms around his neck and pulled him closer for a kiss. Her lips were soft, the touch filled with more love than he could've imagined. Jackson lost himself in the moment, letting everything fall away except this gorgeous woman in front of him. They'd been blessed with a second chance. He intended to savor it.

When the kiss was over, Piper was breathless and her cheeks flushed. She'd never looked more beautiful.

Then she glanced down at the ring. Her eyes widened. "Is that Grandma Mary's engagement ring?"

"Yes. She gave it to me in the hallway just now. She can't wear it anymore because of her arthritis and didn't know what to do with it, but believed God had a plan." He removed the ring from the box. Piper's left arm was in a cast, but thankfully, her fingers weren't swollen from the broken elbow. The diamond band fit perfectly. Jackson chuckled. "She was right. Divine intervention."

Piper looked at the ring on her finger and then at Jackson. Her gaze was soft. "I love you, Jackson."

"I love you too."

He moved to kiss her again, but before he could, the door opened and a nurse walked in with the discharge papers. The next few minutes were spent gathering Piper's things and getting her prescription information squared away. While Piper waited for a wheelchair to take her down, Jackson fetched the car. He pulled his SUV around to the main doors.

Piper rose without a problem from the wheelchair, but she needed assistance getting into the vehicle. Jackson made sure she was comfortable before climbing into the driver's seat. He hesitated. "Are you sure about this? Derek and the ranger team have been working hard to piece together what happened, but they may not know everything. The answers we get may not be the ones you want."

"I know, but with you by my side, I can do anything."

Her words filled him with warmth. Jackson hated to follow up the sweet moment with a meeting at the sheriff's department, but Piper needed answers. She deserved them.

"Okay then. Let's do this."

TWENTY-NINE

Piper wanted to shout about her engagement from the rooftops. Her heart was full, and while she didn't need answers to step into her future with Jackson, it would be nice to finally close this painful chapter of her past. A cool breeze from the air conditioning caressed her cheeks as she limped into the sheriff's department. It was only May, but the days were already heating up. Predictions for a hot summer were probably right.

The bullpen was packed. A fellow deputy spotted Piper and Jackson as they walked in. Cheers erupted as everyone gave them a standing ovation. She limped her way through the crowd, shaking hands and accepting well wishes. Her heart warmed at the friendly faces.

Derek came out of the conference room. His brown eyes shone with affection. "Detective Jensen, it's good to see you on your feet." His use of her official title didn't diminish his greeting. They'd long ago established a way to balance their friendship and professional relationship.

"Ranger Barker." Derek shook Jackson's hand warmly. Then he led them into the conference room.

Felicity and Daniel were seated at the large table with stacks of paperwork in front of them. The whiteboard was covered in dates and notes. Both rangers rose to greet Jackson and Piper. They spent a few minutes chatting about Piper's recovery, and then everyone took a seat.

Jackson moved a chair over for Piper to prop her leg on. The doctor had advised her to keep the foot elevated to help with the pain and swelling. She smiled her thanks and then he claimed the seat next to her. It wasn't professional, but Piper covered his hand with hers under the table. She needed his comforting touch.

He immediately interlocked their fingers and leaned closer until they were shoulder to shoulder.

"We've done a lot of work on the case in the last few days," Derek said, his elbows on the table. Dark circles under his eyes were a testament to the long hours he'd put in. "While we don't know everything, I think we've pieced together everything that happened. Felicity, why don't you start?"

She nodded, making her ponytail bob. "Todd Hutchinson was eighteen years old when he and Lionel Islip made a plan to attack Piper. Lionel had a history of violence against women. He didn't like Piper and blamed her for the breakup with her mother. Todd also had an obsession with Piper, but he wasn't bold enough yet to attack her on his own. He decided to help Lionel by being the lookout."

Her chest squeezed tight. "I didn't know he was there."

"That's because he never entered the house." Felicity's gaze was sympathetic. "There was no way for you to know. Todd, however, could see everything that was happening through the open back door. Emilia did a profile on him, and it's her belief, Todd was inspired by Lionel's attack on you. Five years later, he stalked Debbie Rhodes. She was blonde, blue-eyed, and petite. He kidnapped her from a bar parking lot, took her to a remote wooded area, beat her, and then shot her."

Piper breathed out. "He was reliving the assault on me. But this time, as an active participant."

"Yes. Three years later, he killed Iris Grayson. Same M.O. Last year, Todd was arrested for possession of marijuana. Paul was his attorney. Sometime during the case, Todd told Paul about the murders he committed. Bragging, perhaps?"

"It makes sense." Piper nodded. "Todd created a persona of a drunk dimwit. He didn't have anyone other than his brother to confide in. It wouldn't surprise me if he felt comfortable telling Paul the truth because of attorney/client privilege."

Daniel grunted in agreement. "Paul decided to use Todd's proclivity for murdering blonde-haired, blue-eyed women to get rid of his own problem. Elena."

This much Piper had been able to put together. "Elena and Shawn were in love. Paul was worried that his son would divorce his wife and marry her. He didn't want that. Elena wasn't powerful or connected to a wealthy family. She was undesirable in Paul's eyes. My guess is that he tried to buy Elena off first, but she wouldn't take the money. She and Shawn broke up, but Shawn was so much in love, he kept pursuing her."

"You nailed it. Paul hired Todd to kill Elena. What he hadn't counted on was Todd's obsession with you. The little creep decided it was the perfect opportunity to play a cat-and-mouse game. He killed Elena in the nature preserve, close to the trail where you run. Todd wanted you to find her. Once Jackson arrived in town to help work the case, he took it as a sign that he could finally get his revenge as well." Daniel smirked. "It seems you annoyed him, Barker. He didn't like that Piper preferred you."

Jackson rolled his eyes. "That explains why he tried to blow me up. Several times."

Dark humor, but it made everyone in the room laugh.

"The more things got out of hand, the more nervous Paul became," Felicity said. "He thought Todd would kill Elena, take the money, and leave town. He had no idea Todd had his own agenda until it was too late. Paul tried to control Todd, but that was an impossible feat. As we suspected, Todd used Gerdie to lure Elena out to the woods. Then he killed her too, using her to fuel his game with Piper."

Sick. Piper's stomach swirled with nausea. She didn't want to imagine what poor Gerdie went through. Judging from the grim expressions on everyone else's faces, they were equally appalled.

"How does Marcus fit into all of this?" Jackson asked.

Felicity flipped a pen between her long fingers. "Wally knew what his brother was up to and was worried his obsession would destroy them all. He dosed Marcus with meth, gave him a gun that he'd used in a previous robbery, and then sent him to shoot you. Thankfully he missed, but Paul immediately became concerned Marcus knew too much. He became his lawyer so he could prevent Marcus from talking to us."

"It almost worked."

"Sure did."

"Why was Wally so scared of Paul?"

"Because Paul threatened to tell the police about some crimes they hadn't linked to Wally yet. Like the robbery."

"He did the same with Todd." Piper grimaced. "It didn't go the way Paul planned."

"That explains why Wally demanded protection in exchange for the information he had." Jackson glanced at Piper. "He wouldn't tell us where Todd had taken you without a deal. Lieutenant Rodriguez wasn't having it. Once she had some indication the Kingstons were involved, she had troopers drive by their houses and offices. Wally's truck was spotted in Paul's driveway. That's when SWAT was called in."

Piper was incredibly grateful for the lieutenant's quick actions. It'd saved her life.

"What about Shawn?" Jackson's jaw clenched. "Did he know what his dad and Todd were up to?"

Daniel shook his head. "He didn't have a clue. The emergency he was called away on was legit. A family friend had been in a terrible car accident. Shawn learned about the cabin from Wally. I guess it never occurred to Paul that his son might turn over that information to the police. Additionally, Melanie didn't know about Paul and Todd either. She nearly fainted when she heard the truth. Paul ordered her to keep Wally from talking at all costs. That's why she fought so hard in the hospital room when we went to question him."

Piper sat back in her chair. Her heart hurt for Elena and Gerdie, along with the two other women Todd murdered, but it was a miracle more people hadn't died during this investigation. Three bombs had been detonated. "Where did Todd learn to make the bombs? His brother?"

Daniel nodded. "Along with a little help from the internet." His expression screwed up in disgust. "I'll never understand why clever people use their brains for evil instead of for good."

Everyone in the room nodded in agreement.

Derek leaned forward. "There's good news and there's bad news. The good news is that Paul, Todd, and Wally will never see the outside of a prison cell. The district attorney is throwing every charge she can at them. We have enough evidence to convict them, but I suspect the DA will cut a deal with Paul. He'll testify against Wally and Todd in exchange for life in prison. It will ensure the other two men's convictions."

Piper breathed out. "I'm okay with that."

"The bad news is, if the cases go to trial, you'll have to

testify." Derek's gaze skipped between Jackson and Piper. "Both of you."

They both nodded. Piper squeezed Jackson's hand. She didn't relish the idea of facing Todd down in court, but she'd do whatever was necessary to get justice. Jackson glanced at her and nodded in silent agreement. They would face whatever came together.

As a team.

THIRTY

After the meeting was over, Jackson opened the door to the conference room and was shocked to find his entire ranger team, along with their wives, had joined the sheriff's deputies in the bullpen. Music was playing. Tables along the back wall were loaded down with food and streamers hung from the ceiling. The entire group burst into applause again.

Jackson glanced at Piper. She looked just as shocked as he was.

Derek grinned. "The case is over. It's time to celebrate."

Lieutenant Rodriguez, a soda in hand and a smile on her face, waved them forward. "Don't stand there in the doorway, you two. Come join the fun."

Piper was immediately swept away by Emilia and Felicity. She landed on a chair decorated in colorful streamers. Her smile lit up the room as she chatted with several deputies, along with members of the ranger team.

Jackson's exhaustion eased as he accepted a plate of food and a beverage from Luke. His wife, Megan, was just beginning to show signs of a baby bump. Their second child was due early next year.

"Who planned all of this?" Jackson's gaze narrowed in on Grady and his wife, Tara.

The couple shared a conspiring look. Their daughter, Maddy, giggled with laughter as Elijah and his wife, Sienna, played a card game with her. Luke and Megan's oldest daughter joined the fun.

Tara hitched their son higher on her hip and grinned. "I had the idea, but everyone chipped in to make it happen." She gave Jackson a sisterly hug. "I'm glad you and Piper are okay."

"Thanks."

Not wanting to be far away from Piper, Jackson slowly worked through the crowd to her side. Weston and Avery arrived and brought their newborn daughter with them. Somehow, the infant ended up in Piper's arms. She held the child with a reverence born out of wonder.

Jackson's heart melted. He kissed Piper on the forehead and gazed down at the baby. "She's beautiful."

"She's perfect." Piper blinked as if she was fighting back tears. "A little miracle."

"If you want, you can take that miracle home with you for the night," Avery joked, a teasing grin on her face. She was makeup free, her hair tossed into a messy bun, and there were slight shadows under her eyes from sleeping only a little since the baby was born. Yet every time she looked at her daughter, her whole face brightened. "Let's see what you think at three in the morning. And then at four. And then at five."

Jackson and Piper laughed.

Weston scoffed. "As if Avery could stand to be separated from Charlotte for one night. She can't go five minutes without picking her up. I think the umbilical cord is still attached." His tone was teasing, but there was so much love in his eyes, it was clear he adored how dedicated Avery was to their baby.

"Aunt Piper!" Emma raced up, a bundle of energy and excitement.

Jackson scooped the little girl up before she crashed into Piper and the baby. A stream of giggles followed. Emma grinned. Her top tooth was missing. He pulled back to get a better look and then mimed horror. "Emma, your tooth is gone! Someone call the police. It was stolen."

She shook her head. "No, silly. It fell out."

He screwed up his face in disgust. "It did what?"

"Don't worry. It's a baby tooth. A new one will grow in its place." She touched his cheek. "Yours won't fall out."

Jackson laughed. "I certainly hope not. Otherwise, your Aunt Piper might not think I'm handsome anymore."

"I'll always think you're handsome," Piper said, handing over little Charlotte to Weston. Then she reached out for Emma. "Come give me a hug, sweet girl."

Jackson whispered before setting Emma down, "Be gentle. Aunt Piper still has boo-boos."

Emma nodded seriously and then hugged her aunt with such tender care, Jackson's heart melted all over again. He was turning into a softie. Love must do that.

Finn came over and greeted them, then grabbed his sister to play with some of the other kids. Jackson spotted Ava in conversation with Derek. She laughed and lightly touched his arm. The couple looked very happy together.

A throat cleared. Jackson turned to find Shawn approaching. His muscles tightened involuntarily, but then he forced them to relax. Shawn was hurting too. He'd been deceived, just like the rest of them. Jackson greeted his old childhood friend with a handshake. "Shawn."

"I'm sorry to disturb the party, but I heard Piper had been released from the hospital." Shawn took a deep breath, nerves flashing across his face as his gaze jumped between Jackson and Piper. "I want to apologize. I had no idea what my father had done. He—"

His voice choked off.

Piper rose from the chair and gave him a hug. "You aren't responsible for your father's actions. There's nothing for you to apologize for." She pulled back. "If you hadn't given us the information leading to the cabin, who knows how long it would've taken us to capture Wally and Todd. I'm grateful to you."

Shawn breathed out, obviously overcome with emotion. "That's more kindness than I deserve. Thank you, Piper."

"I hope you and I can bury the hatchet. For good this

time." She wrapped an arm around Jackson's waist. "There's no reason we all can't be friends."

Jackson nodded and clapped Shawn on the shoulder. "I'm sorry for everything you've been through."

"Some of it was of my own making. I've spent a long time in prayer after speaking with my pastor. Melanie and I are going to marriage counseling. We've made a lot of mistakes, and I don't know if things can be saved, but we discovered we want to try. For us and for our kids." His expression hardened. "Now that my father is out of the picture, I think we have a fighting chance."

"I'm glad," Jackson said. "I wish you and Melanie all the best."

"Thanks."

Shawn gave each of them a handshake and then he walked away.

Piper rested her head on Jackson's shoulder. "Do you think they'll make it work?"

He brushed a kiss across her forehead. "I believe in second chances and new beginnings, so yes. If they want it badly enough, with God's help, they'll find a way."

She tilted her head up, and their eyes met. Jackson was transfixed by the love in her eyes. They were in a crowded room of people, but he couldn't resist kissing her. It was light and quick, but his heart still skipped several beats.

"Ugh, get a room." Ava announced as she drew closer, Derek at her side.

Piper laughed, brushing a strand of hair off her forehead. "You are so annoying."

Ava's eyes widened. She grabbed Piper's hand and held it, her mouth dropping open. "Is this an engagement ring?"

Jackson grinned, letting his voice carry across the room. "A room full of law enforcement and it's the civilian who noticed the engagement ring."

Ava squealed with joy and embraced Piper. A crowd gathered to congratulate them. It was a whirlwind of excitement, and hours later, when the party was finally over, Jackson helped his fiancée into the SUV. "Did you have a good time?"

She rested her head against the seat and smiled at him. "The best." She grabbed his shirt and tugged him closer. A mischievous twinkle sparked in her eyes. "But do you want to know what my favorite part was?"

"What?"

"Being with you." She nudged her nose against his. "Kiss me, Barker."

His breath stalled and then he smiled. "You got it, Jensen."

Texas Ranger Heroes Series

Ranger Protection

Ranger Redemption

Ranger Courage

Ranger Faith

Ranger Honor

Ranger Justice

Ranger Integrity

Ranger Loyalty

Ranger Bravery

Triumph Over Adversity Series

Calculated Risk

Critical Error

Necessary Peril

Strategic Plan

Covert Mission

Tactical Force

Would you like to know when my next book is released? Or when my novels go on sale? It's easy. Subscribe to my newsletter at www.lynnshannon.com and all of the info will come straight to your inbox!

Reviews help readers find books. Please consider leaving a review at your favorite place of purchase or anywhere you discover new books. Thank you.